ELECTRIC KISS

THE TURNERS OF COPPER ISLAND
BOOK 4

GRACE HARPER

GRACE HARPER

ELECTRIC KISS

By

Grace Harper

The Turners of Copper Island
Book #4

Electric Kiss by Grace Harper
Copyright © Grace Harper 2023
The right of Grace Harper to be identified as the author of this book has been asserted by the Copyrights, Designs, and Patents Act 1988. Accordingly, copying this manuscript, in whole or in part, is strictly prohibited without the author and her publisher's written permission. It licenses this book for your personal enjoyment only. This book may not be re-sold or given away to other people. If you would like to share this book with another person, please purchase an additional copy for each recipient. If you're reading this book and did not buy it or have not purchased it for your use only, please return it and purchase your own copy. Thank you for respecting the hard work of this author.
All sexually active characters in this work are 18 years of age or older. This is a work of fiction. Names, characters, places, and incidents are solely the product of the author's imagination and/or are used fictitiously, though reference may be made to actual historical events or existing locations. Any resemblance to real persons, living or dead, business establishments, events, or locales is entirely coincidental.

Published by GAVON Publishing, 2023
All rights reserved

✽ Created with Vellum

1

Daisy

Daisy Turner had been back on Copper Island for three months. In those few months, a day hadn't passed without seeing her niece, Isobel. Now that autumn was approaching, Isobel would be in soft squishy onesies, perfect for cuddling. Archer, Daisy's brother and his wife, Erica, had taken to parenthood like they were born to do it.

Daisy had been up since dawn, gone for a run, and returned to shower before she ate breakfast while working on Edward Hall accounts. She and her brothers had started their business mid-way through the financial year while she got work experience after her accountancy qualifications were achieved. It was their first full financial year running the business, and she was keen to make sure everything was in order. That meant she worked every day as it was just her running the money side of things.

Not that she minded.

The four of them had made a commitment to stay

together on Copper Island and run the event business out of Edward Hall. It still surprised her that their aunt had signed it over. Daisy looked through every part of their accounts to make sure they owned every penny they made.

Looking at the clock on her laptop screen, she closed the lid and pushed back on the dining room chair, forgetting it didn't have wheels like her office chair. Groaning, she turned to the side and stood up. Daisy hadn't noticed, but the scents of her childhood had returned with her. Rusty metal and wood, wood smoke, the heat of the fire, and the aroma of sea air, until now.

Remembering that she was in her cottage, she smiled. It was her first home where she didn't have to share a room, bathroom, kitchen, or thoughts unless she wanted to.

Living on Copper Island growing up, there was always someone watching. Then at college and university, she shared housing. When she eventually got onto the rigs, it was even more cramped and no place for solace. The only respite she had was when she and her siblings went travelling the world. Her three brothers shared a room, and she had the other, but she was still with company.

Daisy had always felt the loneliness of being the youngest Turner. They didn't like her at school because of her surname and that she was ahead in her school years. She graduated early from High School. Daisy completed her college diploma in half the time and then passed her engineering degree with flying colours. She wanted to be on the rigs with her dad and brothers.

Working with her dad was short-lived. Two weeks after she arrived on the rigs, he died.

Brain aneurism, dead before he hit the floor. Devastation rippled through her siblings to varying degrees, hitting

Luke the hardest as he was the medic on the rig and felt responsible.

Daisy had a secret weapon, but it didn't fill the loneliness of no one accepting her. She was too bright, too feisty, too accomplished, too happy, and too much of a Turner. She seemed to repel everyone. At school, they mercilessly bullied her as the nerdy girl in a year with girls two years older than her. No one wanted to be her friend. Same for college and then university. It startled Daisy to find there were still men who thought women shouldn't do engineering degrees. When she got to the rigs, it was full-throttle misogyny.

She gave up very early in life, making friends. She hadn't made a single one in her thirty years.

Daisy swiped up her keys from the kitchen counter to her cottage but left her back door unlocked as she walked outside, letting the door close behind her. Her mission wouldn't take long, so she didn't bother locking up after herself. Luke had a habit of coming along to the cottages to make sure they were all locked. He suspected that Aunt Cynthia would come searching for the tin he had found in the warehouse.

She hurried along the dirt path that connected the five cottages. They stood in a row but had a decent amount of space between them. They had privacy.

Daisy had three cottages to her left and one to her right. Her section of the path to Luke and Freya's place was less worn. Dried leaves and twigs crunched under her feet. The path was dirt, unpaved and uneven, like too many birds had dropped their cargo as they flew by.

The autumn leaves scattered over the section from Luke's place to Jason and Heidi's place, but still it was clearer. The nearer she got to Archer and Erica's place, the more debris free and trenched the path became. It was early September, so they were yet to get the miserable mornings of horizontal rain that lashed at her face. She wasn't looking forward to October in the least. Her memories of trudging to and from school leading up to half-term were dire.

In the distance, across the lawns, the ocean crashed against the rocks, the sound calling her to it. The path was rough and worn in places, lined with weeds and tall grass. Daisy hoped they kept the stretch rural. The path she hurried along ran parallel to the cottages. Their homes were on her left and the wide expanse of grass was to her right that led up to fencing and then a cliff. The beach was at the bottom of the sheer drop. The sand was white, and the water on a calm day was clear. With the autumnal weather, Daisy betted it wouldn't be long until the waters were murky as the waves rushed to the shore.

Daisy breathed in the salty sea air. It had a sharp tang to it, like the weather was on the turn. Growing up on Copper Island, she didn't need the weather forecaster or the weather app on her phone. She just needed to smell the air. The cool autumn air was a welcome change from the heat of summer. Daisy would be glad to get back to her cottage.

Freya would be at school, and Heidi, Jason's wife, would be at the surgery. Luke would be at Edward Hall along with Jason, no doubt eating his way through Jason's stores of cupcakes. It did not surprise Daisy that no one was about in their homes. Just because it was Saturday didn't mean they had the day off. Daisy wasn't going into her office at Edward Hall to work, as she had a mission.

Daisy could already smell the rich aroma of fresh coffee that wafted from Archer and Erica's place. The new parents were always up early, even before Daisy awoke.

"Yes," Archer shouted as soon as he clocked her coming

past the wall and onto their back patio. "The baby sitter has arrived."

Archer yawned, then grinned, stood up and stretched tall with his arms above his head like he'd been snoozing. Daisy wouldn't put it past him, as their three-month-old daughter was keeping them awake at night.

Two coffee mugs sat steaming on the squat table. She went straight for the nearest cup.

Archer was dressed casually in long shorts and a long-sleeved t-shirt. He was still barefoot, with his trainers under the table. Another sign he was taking a quick nap.

"Where is Isobel?" Daisy demanded, craning her neck to look through the glass door that led into the kitchen.

Daisy shook her head, her smile widening with each second, excited to see her niece.

"No hello for your brother?" he asked, with fake misery etched across his face.

Daisy rolled her eyes, an amused smile tugging at the corners of her mouth. "Nope. You just called me the babysitter. I want baby cuddles."

Archer sat down to put his trainers on and grinned. He nodded towards the door. "Erica is getting her ready. I've got her bag of stuff here," he said, kicking the oversized bag at his feet by the sofa.

Daisy bent and gave him a hug and cupped his head to kiss it. Then she settled into the nearest armchair, sipping her coffee. She thought it would be a quick handover and regretted not wearing her long woolly cardigan. How Archer could cope with just a t-shirt was crazy. It was a chilly morning.

Smiling widely, she glanced at Archer when he'd finished tying his laces and sat back on the sofa. He slouched and looked in her direction. Her brother looked tired, but happy.

"You're a Dad," she said.

"It's amazing. I can't wait for us all to have kids."

"It will be awhile yet for me. I haven't even seen anyone interesting on the island all summer."

"That's because you haven't left your office all summer."

Daisy winced at his words because he was not wrong. There was a lot of work to be done and now that she was fully qualified and had a few months' experience with Warren Clark as her mentor, she was raring to go. She'd picked accounting practices up easily, much to the amusement of Warren, to the point she was giving him help with his client issues.

"Maybe when the tourists leave, I'll be able to see who lives on the island full time. I don't want to date someone who isn't staying. This is my home now."

Archer gave her a soft smile. "I'm glad you feel that way. I was worried you might not come back and work on Edward Hall accounts remotely."

Daisy drained her coffee mug and placed it back on the table. "Nope. We made a deal, all four of us or none of us."

Archer nodded and closed his eyes as he leaned his head back.

"I am so looking forward to looking after Isobel for the day. She sleeps a lot, right?"

Daisy, until now, had only spent an hour here and there with her niece, but today she had most of the day with her.

"Yeah, pretty much. She's getting stronger every day and likes to grab at things, so you might want to take out your dangling earings."

Daisy's hands flew to her ears, and she pulled out the loops with blue beads threaded through, and put them in her skirt pocket. She had a few curious glances from her work colleagues when she was being mentored at the accountant's firm. Daisy preferred colours and layers. Things that swished and moved. She was born in the wrong decade and could easily fit into the 1970s.

The back door opened, and Daisy and Archer sighed. She suspected for different reasons.

"Oh, here she is. Aunt Daisy is here to spread her sunshine all over you," Erica cooed as she brought Isobel out into the shaded area of the patio.

Erica glowed with health in her plum, long-sleeved maxi dress and white plimsols.

Daisy sprang up, her bracelets jangled as she made her way over to them, grinning at Archer, who continually made fun of her copious amounts of bracelets that made so much noise everyone could hear her coming.

"Isobel likes the noise they make," Daisy said to Archer and poked her tongue out.

"I'll take these down," Archer said.

He stood and lifted the carry cot and bag of tricks.

"Great, the back door is open. We're camping out in the living room," Daisy called out to his back.

Archer lifted a hand in acknowledgement and trudged down the path like a pack horse.

Erica cradled Isobel in her arms, wrapping her in a blanket like the tiny princess she was. Her dark eyes stared up at her mother, watching every expression. She was such a serious and curious baby. The pink blanket kept her snug. Daisy dipped down and kissed Isobel on the cheek, inhaling her baby smells like an addiction.

Erica was fragrant with jasmine, making Daisy feel heady and yearning for another trip to Morocco.

"I'm so grateful you're doing this today," Erica said.

The tip of Isobel's nose was so small, so adorable. That precious pout of hers, not quite a frown, but more a scowl.

Daisy took Isobel and kissed her tiny nose. "It's not a hardship, Erica. I love looking after Isobel. You two deserve a day off and relax. Do you have any plans?"

"Archer has borrowed a boat from Keith, and he's taking me to a cove he knows the tourists don't."

"Sounds perfect. Don't worry about what time you get back. I have plenty of formula and the bottles you made up for me. We'll be fine, and I can lull her to sleep with accountant facts about Edward Hall."

Erica laughed and gave Daisy a hug, with Isobel squished between them.

"It's the first time I'll be away from her all day," Erica said, stroking her daughter's cheek. "I have to get used to being away from her, but it's like I blink, and she develops a little bit more."

Erica was practising her detachment issues before she started her next project.

"When does the movie start?" Daisy asked, while she swayed and cooed at Isobel.

Erica sighed long and hard. "Not for another month, but it will be long days."

"At least you won't have to go far," Daisy said, nodding to Edward Hall. "I bet we'll know they're here with all the noise a movie set creates."

"Yeah, it can be a noisy place, but the grounds are big enough. We hope it swallows up any inconvenience it will cause."

"A minor inconvenience is nothing compared to what it will do for Edward Hall's bottom line. The cottages are far enough away. We won't hear much. There are only a couple of night shoots, so it should all be fine. Don't forget, we all worked on an oil rig. There is no quiet place on one of those."

Erica chuckled. "I am excited to do my first historical film, and on my doorstep. No other locations have I been on have been so near to the set. The morning calls are going to be bliss in comparison."

"Have you convinced Archer to dress like Mr Darcy yet?"

"No, she hasn't, and it won't happen. I'm staying well away from the camera," Archer said, coming into view.

"Spoilsport," Erica said and tilted her cheek for a kiss.

Archer approached and ignored his wife to kiss his daughter's head in Daisy's arms.

Erica pouted, and he relented. He pressed a kiss to her neck and took her hand.

"Come on, honey, we have some relaxing to do," Archer said, tugging on his wife's hand. Then he turned to Daisy as they backed out of the patio. "We'll come and get Isobel later on."

"Don't hurry back on my account. We'll be fine," Daisy said, swaying the baby from side to side. She lifted Isobel's hand to wave goodbye and held her tight.

Erica and Archer walked away hand in hand across the lawn and only looked back once. When they were out of sight, Daisy took a stroll out of the back patio area and wondered if she should go left or right.

"Let's go for a wander before we see Nanny," Daisy whispered against the soft hair on her head.

Daisy wandered back to her cottage and placed Isobel in her carry cot. She then clipped the carry cot onto the pushchair frame and they set off for a walk around the lawn in front of the cottages. It took forty minutes to stroll around and point out wildlife, flowers, and trees. It mesmerised Isobel as Daisy narrated everything she could see. The little girl gurgled as they progressed around the grounds and was sound asleep by the time Daisy reached her back door. Pushing Isobel inside, Daisy settled her, still in her carry cot, on the chair next to where she sat at the dining table.

If she ate with her family, it was around their tables, so she had set up her work station with monitors and laptop in her dining room. Daisy tapped away at her laptop with Isobel sleeping, conducting Edward Hall's accounting business.

There was a message waiting for her from Warren Clark, the accountant who trained her while she was on work experience. Erica had set it up as Warren worked for the accountant's firm, where she held her personal accounts. There were certain perks to working with an entertainment accountant. One of them was many premiere show openings. She spent six months learning all she could from Warren, and her evenings were at events the accountant's firm was attending.

Most of the senior staff had families to go home to, but she was in the city on her own for months, so she grabbed all the tickets. Her wardrobe was filled with dresses, bags, and shoes for every type of event. She would need to create celebrations on Copper Island to get to wear the dresses again. She went alone for half of the events she attended, and for the other half, she went with Warren. He lived in a flat share with three other guys who were seriously into serial dating. Warren told her he was looking for one woman and he'd know her when he saw her.

So he was her platonic date for the events.

Daisy had been back on Copper Island full-time for three months and hadn't seen Warren in person for that time. She missed his company, his easy nature, and his sly wit. Warren's running commentary at the art shows, and movie premiers had her in fits of giggles.

Warren: The office feels empty without you here, filling it with your happy energy. You left me with all the stuffed shirts.

Daisy: They are the same stuffed shirts that were there before I came for job experience.

Daisy smiled. She could see he was answering and sat back, glancing at Isobel to check she was still okay.

Warren: Not really job experience. You showed me a thing or two. Anyway, now you've shown me the colours, I can now only see dull greys.

Daisy: Very poetic. It's gorgeously sunny over here, but autumn is in the air.

Warren: It's raining. Again. It feels like it's been raining for weeks. We're still in summer, and it's miserable.

Daisy: Aww. Copper Island doesn't see full Autumn much later than the mainland. We'll have glorious sunshine until mid-October.

Warren: Show off.

Daisy: You should come over. Surely you can wangle a reason to check up on your tutoring? I bet it will be an expense. Surely Erica needs you to go over her accounts…

Warren: Hmm… maybe. I'll see if it will work.

Daisy: Great. I gotta go, I'm babysitting my niece and crunching numbers before she wakes up.

Warren: All right. Will drop a message when I know I can get over and see what you've been going on about with Copper Island. I'd never heard of it until I met you.

Daisy: It's one of a kind. Speak later. Bye.

Daisy closed the messaging app and worked for another couple of hours. She took care of Isobel, and then it was time for her weekly call.

It was the highlight of her week.

Isobel was awake and alert, meaning Daisy could hold her to the camera.

After making a cup of tea and piling a few biscuits on to a plate, she settled into the armchair in her living room and pulled the table near with her laptop. She then bent to her side, lifted Isobel out of her carry cot, and cradled her in her arms for a cuddle. Daisy was cooing nonsense when her screen came to life.

"Is that my granddaughter?" the woman's voice said.

Daisy grinned at her mum and willed the tears welling to go away.

"Hi, Mum. Yeah. I'm on babysitting duty today."

A sob echoed through the speakers. Daisy looked up and laughed, watching her mother sob into a hanky while she gazed at Isobel.

"She's so tiny," Imelda said, peering closer to her screen.

Daisy lifted the baby up and closer to the camera for Imelda to take a closer look.

"You could hold her if you came to Copper Island," Daisy suggested.

Imelda half laughed, half scoffed at what Daisy said. She did a full roll of her eyes. "I know Cynthia wouldn't let me step one foot on copper Island land. I bet that witch has the ground electrified just for me."

Daisy chuckled, and then Isobel gurgled, showing her gums and blowing bubbles as she moved.

"Oh, she is a darling," Imelda said.

"She is. She's making me broody," Daisy said, kissing Isobel's head and taking a sniff of her baby fragrance.

"Find a husband, and you can have your own."

"Slim pickings on Copper Island when you are persona non grata. I hadn't realised how lonely it is when no one wants to spend any time with me. If it wasn't for the boys' partners, I'd have no female company."

"Is it really that bad?"

"Yeah. Cynthia really has done a number on this island. Everyone hates her. Most of the residents only tolerate us Turners because we give them business. Archer is making headway and Erica helps with her being a superstar actress, but she isn't naïve to think they like her past her being able to get access to stardom."

Imelda's face turned serious, her smile falling away. "Are you doing okay?"

Daisy sighed and hugged Isobel tighter. "Yeah, keeping busy."

"That's not what I meant."

"I know. Stupid things have been triggering me since Luke had the row with Jennifer in the middle of the lawn. If I see something, hear something or experience something, I freeze and can't shake off the fear. Like an hour ago, I saw this toy, and I went cold all over and spaced out."

"What toy, honey?" Imelda said softly.

Daisy jostled an alert Isobel to reach into her carry cot for the soft toy that had seen better days. She held it up to the camera. Imelda held her hand over her mouth, but Daisy heard the gasp.

"I bought that for you. It used to be in the playroom you all shared," Imelda said.

"I don't remember it and I don't know why. We found it with boxes of toys in the warehouse the boys were clearing out for Erica's venture."

"The bunny's ears have faded a bit, but Freddie said you and that rabbit were inseparable for years."

Daisy gave it a closer look, jostling it from side to side to make Isobel's eyes light up. She turned to look back at her mum.

"That must be it, but why would I be so fearful at seeing it?"

"I don't know, honey. I'd gone by that stage."

They fell into a silence. Daisy hated talking about anything that made her mother remember she lost out on so many years with her children.

"You could come back… come and stay in the spare cottage and we could be a family again."

"You know I can't do that, honey, while Cynthia is still alive. I'm not sure Archer, Jason and Luke would welcome me with open arms either. They think I abandoned them."

"Well, I know the truth and if I have to, I will make the old cow admit what she did in front of them so you can come back."

"That's kind of you, but it would make me feel better if you weren't within a hundred feet of that woman."

"I try not to be. I go to the kitchens because Maggie and Bailey are good people, but as for her. I don't wish to see her again."

"Tell me how Warren is. Do you get to see him since you're back on the island?"

Daisy let her change the subject, but not without warning in her voice.

"Mum…"

"What? He's a nice guy."

Imelda tried to look innocent, but it wasn't working.

"He's just a friend."

"He looks like you're the best meal he'll ever have."

"Mum!"

It always shocked her when her mum showed any

interest in who liked her, forgetting that she must be lonely too after a decade of being a widow.

"I'm not that old, honey. I know what lust and admiration look like. I'm still in my sixties."

"You don't look it. You look far younger."

"Thank you, darling. Now, I'm going to let you go because your old mother needs a disco nap before she heads out to dinner with some friends."

"All right, mum. I'll speak to you next week. I love you."

"I love you too, honey."

Daisy ended the session and cuddled Isobel closer, thinking back to why she was scared to see an old toy of hers. She didn't truly understand why she wouldn't go beyond the kitchens of Turner Hall, either. If it wasn't for Maggie and Bailey, she wouldn't go near the place.

"Shall we go to see if Jason's home? Maybe your aunty can blag a dinner and escape making dinner for one again."

Isobel gurgled her reply, and Daisy nodded at her affirmation. She bundled up the little girl, and they took a stroll to her brother's place. Luke and Freya were in the kitchen with Heidi around the kitchen island when she tapped on the glass door. Heidi's eyes lit up when she saw Isobel.

"Oh, come in," Heidi said, with her hands outstretched for Isobel.

"You're only happy to see me because I have this bundle of joy," Daisy said with a grin.

"And you're only here so you don't have to cook," Jason said from the stove.

"That is true," Daisy said and laughed.

"Pull up a chair. We're wondering how long Archer and Erica can stay away until they buckle and want to see their child."

"I'm shocked I didn't get a visit already," Daisy said, accepting the glass of wine Heidi passed to her.

Jason continued to prepare dinner while Daisy, Freya, and Heidi fussed over the little one. Luke stood hip to counter with a beer in his hand, chatting to Jason as he chopped and diced the ingredients. Ten minutes later, Archer and Erica approached the back door and pushed the door open looking fresh faced and happy. Their eyes moved immediately to Isobel.

Luke looked at his watch. "I win, pay up," Luke said to Jason.

2

Nate

Nate had been running his boat repair shop for a little over six years. His father had opened the shop when Nate was a young boy, and it had always been a dream of Nate to continue the tradition. Some days, however, it seemed like a thankless endeavour.

No one ever seemed to come by. It was heart-breaking. He opened the shop doors faithfully every morning, hopeful that the day would bring some business. He had a few regulars, but they were few and far between. Nate resigned himself to his own lonesome company, filling the space with boat parts and tools.

Despite being a lone wolf, the idea of finding a wife fascinated Nate. In his more honest moments, he wished for his father to come back. To share the joys of boat repair with him, a fellow enthusiast who could appreciate the beauty of his trade. He wanted someone to chat with, to share stories, and to laugh with. His father had moved off Copper Island with his mum six years ago when he could see the business was slowing down. Cynthia had systematically run the island like she didn't care. His mum and dad regularly offered him a job at the mechanic's workshop on the mainland, where plenty of business fixing boats were on the harbourside.

Nate wanted to stay on Copper Island. He liked island life.

Still, without fail, Nate opened the doors of his shop every morning with a smile on his face. He was determined to keep his father's business alive and didn't plan on giving up anytime soon.

Nate had always been a bit of an introvert, so the solitary nature of his job didn't bother him too much. In fact, he was often content to just sit in the workshop's corner, tinkering away at whatever project he had set his mind on. He enjoyed the peace and quiet, taking solace in the fact that he was working towards a greater goal.

With the passing of time, Nate developed an affinity for his new place of work. After all, it was his, and he was proud of the progress he had made. He had slowly but surely transformed the shop into a haven for boat repair.

Nate took in the details of his workspace, noticing the small things like the creaky floorboards, tatty yellow armchair and the pungent oil smell. He had become so familiar with the space that it almost felt like a second home. Even in the silence, he could find solace and comfort from his labours.

Nate boiled the kettle and made a cup of strong tea. Snatching up the packet of chocolate digestives still in the packet, he went to the side opening of his workshop and shouldered the door open to a smaller workspace. In the centre was his prized possession, his Kawasaki GPZ750.

There wasn't much road on Copper Island, but he wanted a project to work on with all his downtime and to learn to restore something other than boats.

He had to diversify if he wanted to stay. His revenue was down so much from the previous year, he was grateful he no longer needed to pay any taxes, or so he hoped.

A bang on the door brought him out of his thoughts an hour later. His best mate, Selly, stuck his head around the door.

The door was ajar, a sliver of light between the door and door frame. Selly's face was one of concern and intrigue. A hint of grease and gas, the smell of warm oil, and the aroma of pollen carried in the wind wafted around as he pulled the door open wider. The door's hinges creaked as Selly eased it open.

"Hey, Nate. You coming out tonight?"

"Maybe. What time is everyone meeting?"

"About eight in the pub," Selly said, taking a closer look at the bike Nate was working on. "You finished it yet?"

"I can't ride it yet, but it's not far off."

"It's looking good. How's business?"

Selly, his friend since school, was a florist. He had a piece of land as part of his parents' property and grew tulips, then shipped them to the mainland. Unless they had a freak weather front, Selly's business wasn't likely to go quiet. Not even Cynthia Turner could spoil the flowers.

"Slower than normal."

"Don't forget to phone that free helpline. They'll be able to help with the tax questions."

"I will. I'll do that soon."

"Make sure you do. It will be one less thing to worry about. I'll see you at the pub. First round's on me," Selly said and then was gone.

3

Daisy

Daisy sat up in bed wondering when she should learn how to operate her heating. The mornings were getting cooler and her tank and PJ shorts weren't keeping her warm like they had over the summer. The mug of tea sitting on her nightstand was steaming hot as she tapped away on her laptop. Her head snapped up when she heard her back door open and then shut.

She'd forgotten again to lock her back door. If that was Luke coming in, she was in for a telling off for not staying safe. The thud of feet told her it was Archer and Teddy.

Archer's stray dog was home.

"You decent?" Archer called out from the hallway when he'd reached the top of the stairs.

Teddy clearly didn't care if she was decent or not as he ran into her bedroom and jumped up at the side of the bed. Daisy looked at the clock on her screen and thought for a moment she was running late, but it said seven o'clock.

"Yeah, I'm decent," she called out, putting her laptop to one side and patting the duvet for Teddy to jump up.

Archer came to the doorway and laughed at Teddy, trying and failing to get up. Daisy leaned forward and clutched him under her legs and yanked him up. He rewarded her with doggy kisses, which she tried to keep to her jaw and neck.

"You're up early?" she said as she dodged Teddy left and right.

"Yeah, taking Teddy for his morning walk and thought I'd test out your back door. I wasn't shocked to find that it wasn't locked. You look like you've been up a while. Is that tea still warm?"

Daisy widened her eyes at Archer's series of questions, choosing to acknowledge the last one.

"Yeah, I haven't had any yet if you want it."

Archer strolled over to the table, strode with his heavy boots and picked up the mug. He carried it back to the chair in the corner and flopped down. Leaning back, he balanced the ceramic mug on the arm and whistled for Teddy. The dog didn't move from his warm spot under the covers but glanced at Archer, then Daisy. His ears pinned back slightly as he yanked his nose under the duvet and snuggled deeper into her bed.

Teddy broke his habit of getting over excited and calmed down. After months of training with a handler, he was like a new and mature dog. Teddy had become well-behaved in how he acted around people, especially Archer and Erica's baby.

Archer groaned as he eyed Teddy's uncooperative behaviour. "I've only had him back one day, and he's already defying me."

Daisy smiled warmly at Archer, looking amused by the situation. "The trainer said he'll be okay with Isobel?"

"Yeah," Archer answered, still watching the dog with a furrowed brow. "It was worth all those months being away to get him child friendly. I remember the dogs we had around the estate when we were little. I don't even know whose they were. They were just Turner dogs, but I enjoyed having animals."

Daisy's expression shifted to longing, and she said dreamily, "I'd like a cat."

Archer snorted in response. "Cats are arseholes, no loyalty," he declared, before draining his cup of tea.

"Yeah, true, but I like their attitude."

Archer barked out a laugh at Daisy's comment.

"So, why are you up so early?" he asked.

"Doing Edward Hall stuff. Want to get a routine, so we're shipshape for auditors and tax inspections. I'd rather get things sorted as we go than have to do them at the end of the tax year."

"Do you really have to get up so early for that?"

"I guess the rigs have me in an early routine and then working at the accountant's firm. It was long days while I was learning. Kinda used to it, plus there is not much else to do."

"All right, but the point of us all working together is that we work together to make our lives easier, not harder. We've had enough of that."

"If it gets too much, I'll come and see my big brother," Daisy said and grinned.

Teddy had inched himself to Daisy's lap and had his head leaning on her thigh, which she scratched behind his ears.

"You do that, sis," he said and stood.

Archer came over, kissed her head and left the empty tea mug on her nightstand.

"If I come by tomorrow on the morning walk and find your door open, I am ratting you out to Luke. Lock your door, Daisy."

Archer let out a command, and Teddy leapt off the bed and joined Archer, sitting on his backside and thumping his tail. It impressed Daisy that a simple noise had the dog to heel.

"He's obedient," Daisy remarked.

"He is. No feeding him any treats."

"Would I?" she said in mock affront, with her palm on her chest.

"I fully expect there to be a glass jar with a flip-top lid with doggy treats within days somewhere in this house."

"Aww Archer, how am I supposed to spoil him?"

"Buy a cat," he said, laughing as he left her alone.

Daisy waited for her back to close and then sank back onto her pillows. She didn't display any mementoes or personal items she'd collected over the years. They were still in boxes in the spare bedroom. She mused when the time would come that she didn't want to bolt. Telling Archer that she was all in was one thing. Telling her addled mind was another.

"I'm totally getting a cat," Daisy muttered.

She reached for her mug of tea and forgot her brother had drunk it. Thumping the empty mug down, she threw back the duvet and headed for the bathroom. She might as well start her day.

Once she showered and dressed, Daisy grabbed her laptop bag and headed to Edward Hall. Only Erica was at home reading a pile of papers that looked like lines for a movie with Isobel at her feet in her carry cot. Daisy didn't have time for baby cuddles, and Erica looked deep in thought, so she carried on walking to Edward Hall.

They didn't have any groups staying at the hall that week, so the place was eerily quiet. Heading for her office on the ground floor, she entered the building through the front door. The enormous wooden doors creaked as she shouldered her way in. If they had paying groups, the main doors were wedged open. But she tended to go through the kitchens if there were residential groups. That morning she wanted to avoid pastries and bacon if she wanted to stay fit. After six months in London and three months at Edward Hall, she noticed she wasn't as toned as before. She needed to get back out on her surf board. The sea was getting more turbulent as the season wore on, so there weren't many weeks left she could go out. The perfect solution would be to swim laps in the pool at Turner Hall, but being watched by her aunt sent shivers down her back. There had to be another way to stay fit.

Daisy pushed down the handle of her office door and shouldered it open. It was a decent size, and like all rooms in Edward Hall, it had tall ceilings with windows overlooking the grounds. Her office was across the foyer, down a short hall on the ground floor. She had the perfect view when groups would work out on the lawns. Freya would sneak in and gawp once she'd found out where Daisy's office was positioned. Freya was now engaged to Luke, so it was a moot point, or so Freya let Luke think. There were times when Daisy got an unexpected visit from Freya for no reason at all that coincided with a session on the lawns with half-dressed men.

Daisy hadn't made it homely yet, but she had dragged in a plant from outside to the left of the window that allowed her to spy the outside without being seen. Other than the tall potted plant, there was a desk that had seen better days and was older than her aunt. A squeaky chair on wheels that was around the same date as the desk, a blue rug that ran to an inch of all four walls and two functional chairs on the opposite side of the desk. She had a fancy monitor to which she could hook her laptop and a chipped mug filled with pens and pencils.

That was the sum total of her office. No pictures, no filing cabinets, and nothing to give it any personality.

She vowed to add more things as the months wore on. One item on her list was a kettle, a small fridge for milk and a jar for her tea bags. But for now, she wandered down to the kitchens with her travel mug and stole Jason's stash. She rounded the desk, put her laptop back on the floor, and grinned at the round foil-covered dome in the centre of her desk.

"So much for giving up bacon," she said aloud, picking up what she knew was a bacon bap.

Jason arranged for breakfast to be waiting for her on her desk before she arrived every day. She loved her brother for it. He recognised she worked long hours for the greater good of all four of them. When he'd quizzed her a couple of weeks into her permanent position, when she came skulking for food, he said he would feed her breakfast and lunch while at Edward Hall. She could join his table for dinner if she didn't feel like cooking.

Daisy worked through the whole day, only stopping when Jason brought her a sandwich for lunch, and then she was on her way home. All the cottages for her brothers had lights on, but no one was outside. So she carried on to her place, thinking of the bath she'd promised herself if she'd got her to-do list done.

Turning the handle on her back door, she huffed when it

wouldn't open. She cursed Luke and rooted around in her laptop bag for her keys. She cursed some more when she found them, and an errant paperclip dug in under her nail. Daisy simmered instantly, thankful she had brothers who cared about her safety. Leaving the laptop back on her dining table, she kicked off her shoes into the cupboard under the stairs and then ran up to the first floor taking the stairs two at a time. Daisy had about an hour before she needed to get online for her volunteer work. She was one of many accountants that helped start-ups with basic accounting questions. A lot of them were sole traders. She wanted to set one up for Copper Island but wasn't sure how that would go down as the Turner siblings hadn't received open house invitations from many of the residents since they'd returned home.

Still, it was on her list of things to accomplish to give back to the island, to balance out the damage Cynthia had done over the years.

After a while, Daisy got out of the bath and wrapped herself in a towel before sitting down with her laptop. She pulled on her headset, dialled into the network, and waited for her calls to come through. It didn't take long before one came connected. Daisy took a deep breath and answered.

"Hi, this is Daisy. How can I help?"

"Uh, hi. I wondered if you could give me some advice?"

The caller's voice was deep and rumbly. She found listening to those few words enough to want to know everything about him. He sounded intense but knew exactly what he wanted.

Daisy cleared her throat and waited a moment before speaking.

"Sure, I'll help where I can, and if I can't, I'll find

someone who can. What is the problem?" Daisy asked, her voice gentle yet professional.

"My business has been running well for several years, but this last couple of years has seen a massive downturn, and I wondered if I could get out of paying the extra 50% in advance tax."

"Sure, you can appeal to HMRC, but you need to be careful it's not a temporary blip because if your business does have an upturn, HMRC will think you're trying to pull a fast one."

The man's voice sighed long and hard. "I doubt that's going to happen if the last six years are anything to go by. Ever since old man Turner died, this island has gone to ruin."

Daisy's heart stilled. She was talking to an islander, and he was referring to her grandfather.

"What kind of business do you run?"

"I'm a boat mechanic. My Dad moved off the island and said I could go with him, but I stayed and took over the family business while he went to the mainland and started fresh. He's doing well, but there aren't many boats that need fixing where I live. Fewer boats are coming to the island, meaning fewer boats need fixing. With fewer people coming to visit the island, there are fewer mouths to feed. With fewer mouths to feed, fewer boat trawlers needing fixing as they're not going out to catch fish."

"Right, it sounds like a spiral. Can you diversify?"

"Not really. I only know about boats."

"Well, I hope the new generation can turn things around if the... what did you call him?"

"Old Man Turner. He wasn't a nice guy, which probably accounts for his not very nice daughter, who hides away and has no interest in the island. It's like having a CEO of a company who doesn't give a shit. The thing is, I love living on this island, but there'll be a time when I'll have to move to the mainland too. Maybe my father had it right."

A silence fell between them. Daisy wondered if he remembered her name at the beginning of the call. Not many did, and she hoped he hadn't too. There wasn't much she could say without revealing she knew which island he was talking about or who she was. He filled the silence for them.

"You don't need to hear about my issues. I'm sure you hear all the sob stories on this line. I'll let you go. Thanks for the advice. I'll give it some thought before I call the tax man."

"Okay, well, we're here if you need more advice."

"Thanks." She could hear the smile in his voice. "Have a great evening. I'm off to get some fish and chips."

"Sounds like a perfect evening," she replied.

The call ended, but not before she heard his laugh. It was deep and rumbly, and what she wouldn't give to feel that rumble wrapped up in his arms.

Daisy was keen to look up the boat mechanics on the island and search out fish and chip shops. She could take a walk into town and wander about.

Looking at the clock on her screen, she had another two hours of hotline calls, and then it would be too late to eat. She'd save her sleuthing for another evening. She wanted to hear his laugh in person.

Even if he hated the Turners.

4

Nate

Nate had an hour before he needed to take the boxes to the far end of the quay. It was a side hustle he had, as the only forklift truck on the island belonged to Hill's Workshop. As Nathaniel Hill, he was the only one to drive it. Not that there was anyone else on the island who was qualified to handle a forklift vehicle.

He was on his back tightening up a nut on the motorcycle wheel one-handed. The ache in his wrist resting on his stomach reminded him he needed to see the doctor the following morning.

His phone rang. It was on the floor next to him, just in case a potential customer needed his expertise. Nate instructed his phone to answer when he saw who it was.

"Hi, Dad. How's it going?"

The view from the video screen is of a kitchen, slightly out of focus. His dad was standing in front of a silver fridge with the phone propped up against the coffee jar. Nate knows this because the conversation is always the same.

His mum's voice could be heard in the background.

"Yes, I'm talking to Nate... no, I haven't used the easel for the phone. The coffee jar is perfectly fine..." Then his father let out a sigh. The phone jostled and then was placed a little higher than before.

"Our son looks fine. Proof of life confirmed," his father shouted.

Then there was quiet and a loving, exasperated glance over his dad's shoulder, and then he returned his focus to Nate.

His father's eyes crinkled at the sides, and his hair was dark with grey streaked through, cropped short, parted just off centre and combed neatly to the side.

"Hello, Son. As you can hear, nothing has changed at this end. We're busy as ever. I thought I'd give you a call to see how you are."

"I'd like to say I'm busy too, but it's slow going."

"You'd make quicker work of that, but if you used both hands," his dad quipped, nodding to Nate's bike.

Nate sighed, wishing he hadn't accepted the video call. It wouldn't be long before his mum was on the call asking why he wasn't using both hands. He decided to be straight.

"I got hit yesterday. My wrist is a little swollen."

"Rowing, I bet. I swear you get more injuries doing that sport than getting past the winning post."

His father was laughing. It was Hill lore that Nate wasn't great at rowing, but he stayed on the team to keep fit when they trained. He was never in the boat when they competed.

"I'll get it looked at. Let Mum know I'm not at death's door."

"Will do, Son. Do you have any bookings?"

"None. I'm doing more business shifting boxes around the island on the truck than I am fixing boats. I called the financial tax helpline, and they said I could request not to pay next year's advance payments. The woman said to be sure business wouldn't pick up and make me look like I was trying to pull a fast one with the tax man."

His father's face dropped its joviality and turned serious. "What do you think the chances are over there?"

"There is definitely potential. Archer Turner seems to be making some changes. Their business always has events booked in, meaning knock on business for the town, but not many come by boat."

"If the events increase, then the ferry boats will increase, and you know how often they break down and need fixing before they head back out again. My advice is to give it another year. Then if things don't pick up, you'll have more than the tax bill to consider. If you decide to come to the mainland, you will always have a job with me. You know that, right?"

His dad had his arms folded across his chest, dropping his chin to illustrate he meant every word. Nate felt the love and support through the phone. His parents had always given him their unwavering support and encouragement. Nate's dad meant everything he was saying and had demonstrated it his entire life.

He tried not to sound defeatist, but it was hard.

"Yeah, Dad, but I love living on Copper Island, even if it isn't the same as it used to be."

"I get that, and I'm proud you're giving it your all. What are you doing to pass the time?" his dad asked.

"I bet he spends his nights reading," Nate's mum chipped in.

"Hi, Mum. Yeah, have been doing some reading."

"I knew it. Don't forget to invite us over soon. I miss your face," she said.

Nate rolled to his side and switched to give her his full face on the video.

"It's not very pretty at the moment," Nate said, grinning, knowing he had oil smears across his cheek.

"My handsome son. Why hasn't someone snapped you up yet?" she asked, giving him a cheesy smile.

"I'm choosy," he replied.

"Don't be a stranger. The ferry goes both ways," his mum chastened and then blew him a kiss. "Gotta check on dinner."

Nate watched his mum flick the towel at his dad's legs and then run off. His parents were as in love as he had ever seen them.

He wanted that.

"Tell me what you're doing with the bike?" his dad asked.

"It's nearly done. There aren't any long stretches of open road to test it out, but I'll have a ride around the island."

"Don't forget the runway. The flights stop early. You could always ask them if you can use the strip for a test run."

Nate brightened. "That's not a bad idea."

"Not just a hat rack," his dad said, pointing to his temple.

Nate laughed at his dad's old joke. He missed his parents and their easygoing nature. They were forgiving in that they moved on from whatever troubled them. When Old Man Turner died, and they decided to move off the island, there was no malice or resentment like some of the islanders, just practicality.

Nate was one of them that harboured resentment at Cynthia Turner and her lack of attention to what was happening on her island.

"I need to get ready to take the load to the boat. I earn more money driving the forklift than fixing boats these days.

"Gotta diversify where you can, Son," his dad said wisely.

Those words he'd already heard from the accountant on the phone came back to him. Her voice had played around in his head for days, and he wanted to hear it again. Nate needed to let his dad go. Otherwise, he was likely to talk himself into selling the business. Yet, deep down, Nate knew he had to stay for another year. He didn't know why, but somewhere, his mind was telling him to hang on a little longer.

"True. You taught me that. I'll need to get to my boxes. I'll call you soon," Nate said, lifting his good hand to say goodbye.

"Take care, Son," his dad said, and the screen went blank.

The sound of a boat engine rumbled in the distance, and blades of harsh white light sliced through the open garage door, no doubt from a tug boat in the harbour.

He slumped onto the concrete, the chill of the floor seeping into his body. Nate stared at the metal beams that kept the garage upright in the roughest storms, reminding him of the silent strength that held his world together.

He thought of the long wheelbarrow waiting to be loaded with boxes of scraps, the forklift to be driven out into the night as he took the salvaged metal pieces to the cargo boat. In the back of his mind, a faint voice told him he could take a break and go for a quick shower and off to the pub for a pint. But then the voice faded away, replaced, knowing that he couldn't forgo the money. Evenings like these always seemed to have too little to do and too much time to do it.

Rising to his feet, he dusted off his clothes and reached

for the hose nearby. He took a few moments to clean his face and hands before clearing away his tools. He'd get a pint later, he thought to himself, but for now, he had to get to work.

5

Daisy

*D*aisy had an evening free and was looking for company. Luke, Jason and Archer, with their significant others, were busy. Otherwise known as a collective early night, she noted as she walked along the path past their cottages. The evenings drew in so she could detect the lights on and in which rooms, as all the cottages were identical.

The rumbly laugh played on repeat in her head for the last week since she took the call from the boat mechanic, who she now knew was Nathaniel Hill. Light internet stalking gave her that much.

Daisy was disappointed that it was him. She didn't have fond memories from school of Nate and his mates. But then, no one was kind to her through school.

It was Friday evening, and she wanted fish and chips. She'd wanted fish and chips since he'd mentioned it on the call. It had nothing to do with the off-chance of looking for the mechanic's boat workshop.

Daisy had not used the golf buggy parked at the end of the pathway with her coloured bench seat often since she'd moved back to the island permanently. She toyed with the idea of driving into the town because the fish and chips would be warmer by the time she got back, but it was a lovely warm evening.

After a back and forth in her head, she decided not to take the buggy and walk down to the quayside. Instead, she took the private Turner path and ended up at the small port where the tug boats moored up. Then she walked through the town and out the other side to where the Turner warehouse was. She knew there was a fish and chip shop at the end of that quay. What she also knew from some online searching was where the only boat mechanic had its workshop.

She might have checked out Hill's Workshop a time or two, hoping to see what her caller looked like now he was an adult and not a spotty teenager. Unfortunately, the only pictures on the website were of boats in dry docks.

The sun had started to set, bathing the waterfront in a soft golden glow that seemed to reflect off the surface of the still water. The shadows stretched along the wide quay, lengthening the already impressive warehouses and workshops that lined the shore.

As she walked, she could hear the gentle lapping of water against the wooden posts and the clang of a distant bell ringing out from a freight boat. She passed a few people, but no one paid her any mind as she made her way to the Turner warehouse.

On the pretence of checking that the warehouse was locked up, knowing that Archer would have ensured it was secure, she strolled along the wide quayside towards the workshop. The place was between her and the Turner warehouse. With every step, the air felt heavier, and she felt a strange sensation in her stomach, a mixture of anticipation and fear.

Finally, she reached the wide doors that led to the workshop. Pausing for a moment, she took a deep breath and looked inside.

It startled her as she approached the open garage doors to Hill's Workshop and saw the interior lights blazing with a radio blaring. As she approached the opening, she saw a glimpse of a battered mustard-coloured armchair, and she froze, transported back to a time her mind was suppressing. It was like she was seeing a snippet of time that she never knew existed.

Daisy shook her head, vaguely aware that her earrings had caught in her hair. The pain was excruciating as she shook violently on the spot, and she could feel tears streaming down her cheeks. She tried to catch her breath but instead felt overwhelmed by the deep sadness of her childhood.

Suddenly, it felt like time had stopped. All the sights and sounds around her faded away as she found herself transported back to a memory she had been suppressing for years.

She was six or seven years old again, standing in a room in Turner Hall, bawling at the top of her lungs. She heard shouting and felt something inside her breaking as another crash reverberated around her. Daisy wasn't sure if the noise was her memory or real life. It was like she was blinded to reality and stuck in her past.

Daisy was terrified.

And just as suddenly as it began, the trance broke, and

Daisy gasped for air as she realised where she was standing —outside Hill's Workshop at dusk. She looked around frantically before clapping a hand over her mouth.

Daisy slowly stepped forward, feeling a chill run down her spine. In front of her, she found a man lying on the ground with his face contorted in pain. He was wearing a dirty white tank top with green overalls unbuttoned to the waist. His entire body was shaking with each breath he took.

"What the hell is wrong with you?" he shouted out. "Didn't you hear me?"

She didn't respond, too paralysed by fear to move or speak. To her relief, the man seemed to not notice as he shifted onto his back and groaned in agony.

The light from the quayside lamp above illuminated his face, and Daisy knew immediately who this man was— Nathaniel Hill. He was older but still had the boyish features she remembered from school.

He looked up at Daisy with pain in his eyes, but something else was behind them. Despite how weak he appeared right then, determination and strength seemed to radiate from him.

"Can you help me? I think I need to get up," he said in a pained voice. "I think I've done something to my arm."

Daisy looked at the man on the floor, his shoulder twisted at an ugly angle. Then, moving into rescue mode, she hoisted her skirts and tucked them into her waistband, creating Buddha-style trousers. Squatting, she hefted the wheelbarrow upright, then crouched near the man and saw he was the most handsome scowly man she had ever seen. That was a big statement, as she had worked with hundreds of scowly men on the rigs.

"Are you all right?" she asked.

He looked up, his face twitching slightly as he mustered

a feeble smile. "I think I've broken something," he muttered as he drew his eyebrows together, giving her the once over.

"Stop checking me out while I see what damage you've caused."

"One, I'm not checking you out, and second you caused the damage," he said.

"How fast were you going that you couldn't stop pushing this wheelbarrow?"

Nate winced and looked sheepish.

"It isn't a wheelbarrow. It's a trailer with handles I adapted. It doesn't turn left or right just goes straight. I'm not used to anyone being down here, so I thought it was safe to free-wheel it."

"I see," she said, not looking at his face but carefully pressing her thumbs into his shoulder to see if he had broken anything or was being a big baby. She'd had some experience of that, too, on the rigs. Her brother Luke gave her basic training for first aid over the years, so she knew a thing or two about breaks, sprains and dislocations.

This man had managed to dislocate his shoulder. Which was amazing, seeing as he couldn't have been going that fast.

The man's face was stubble covered, and his grey eyes were soft. They twinkled in the light of the quayside lamps. His lips were full, his hair was thick and dark, and his body was tall, brawny and broad.

"Why were you just standing there? And why couldn't you hear me?" Nate asked, struggling to sit up.

Daisy scurried to his back. "It doesn't matter. Can you sit up?"

"Yeah," he muttered.

"Come on, you big burly baby, get some brave pants on," Daisy said to him.

The man smelled of oak with a hint of oil.

There it was, that rumbly laugh, and she had her palm on his back, feeling it through his ribs. She got him to a sitting position, and his eyes scanned her face, then her body and then her bare legs. She had a lot on show when she stuffed her skirts between her legs and into the back of her waistband. It was the easiest way to ride a bicycle. It was her preferred mode of transport when they travelled abroad, and she got used to the practicality if she didn't want to trip over.

Daisy narrowed her eyes into slits. "Didn't I mention earlier to stop checking me out?"

Another rumbly laugh. His handsome face came alight when he smiled. It was almost enough to take her breath away.

"Sorry," he muttered but not looking the least bit remorseful.

"Let's get you up and see what the damage is. My guess is it's a dislocation."

"You a doctor?"

"Ha! No, far from it, but I know a fair bit of medical emergency stuff."

She helped him up with his good arm and circled him so she was at his front. She pushed and prodded, and with the yelps he let out, she knew for sure he had dislocated his shoulder. Which meant it needed to be put back in place. She'd done a few on the rigs but doubted this man would let her do it. He seemed the proud independent type.

Daisy stood face to face with him, her hands on his upper arm and shoulder.

"Okay. Bad news, you've dislocated your shoulder," Daisy said, grinning up at him.

"Why are you smiling at that? It fucking hurts."

"Well, you'll think twice next time you think about speed and freewheeling like you're at the supermarket and want to have fun with the trolley. I'm smiling because there's good news."

"Which is? You know a doctor?" Nate asked, wincing from the pain.

"Well, I do know a medic, but I can fix this for you."

"Oh no, a tiny thing like you? Nope."

Nate was backing away, a little fear on his features as he gave her another once over.

"I'm not that tiny. My brother makes the most delicious cakes."

"Compared to me, you're tiny. What are you? Five foot three?"

Nate looked down at her, his eyes were changing from grey to blue, but it was her mouth he couldn't stop staring at.

He cleared his throat and looked over her shoulder.

"I'm five feet seven, thank you very much. I just look tiny compared to your six feet."

Daisy moved forward, seemingly chasing after him. She had met men like him before who didn't want her to fix them.

They stood face to face, her hands on his upper arm and shoulder. She could feel the warmth of his body through his shirt.

"Okay," she said, her voice soft and soothing. "You're going to be brave. There is no point staying in pain when I can make it go away. Don't be stubborn."

Nate seemed to contemplate what she was saying, still not giving in.

"I can help you if you want," Daisy said, her gaze still

locked with his. "It's going to hurt, but it'll be quick, and it'll get you fixed up."

Her voice was so calm, her words hopefully comforting.

"Six feet one, I think you'll find," he muttered.

Daisy rolled her eyes and laughed. "Like an inch matters," she scoffed and then felt herself go red.

She resisted the urge to lift her hands to her cheeks to see if they were burning as much as they felt.

"I think we both know every inch counts," he said so low she felt it in her stomach.

Desperate to not think of this man naked, she closed her eyes for two seconds and then opened them again.

"All right, let's get this over with," Daisy muttered. She cleared her throat. "Ready?"

"How do you want me?" he asked.

She didn't miss his smirk.

It was then she realised they hadn't exchanged names.

"Don't you mean where do I want you?"

"Whatever," he said, shrugging his bad shoulder and wincing.

"Okay, have you got a desk-type chair in your workshop?"

"Yeah, I'll get it."

"Why don't you stay here, and I'll get it?"

Nate nodded, and she strode a few paces before turning.

"Where am I going to get it?"

"Far left-hand corner, try not to trip over anything."

"I'll try to navigate my way around a spanner." She said wearily.

His rumbly laugh left her hot and bothered as she ventured into the workshop. She pulled her skirts free as she walked and side-eyed the yellow armchair. She wasn't sure why seeing it caused her to freeze. Daisy whipped out her phone and snapped a picture to ask her mum the following day. If the toy had a reason, then the armchair might too. She found the chair covered in oil smears and brought it back outside. He looked at her legs, and his face fell. She smiled at his disappointment they were back under cover. He liked her.

"You got a name?" Daisy asked as she swung the chair around and pointed to the seat.

He sat down and looked up. "Nathaniel. You?"

"Daisy," she replied.

"Suits you," he said.

Daisy smiled, brought the wheelbarrow over to where he was sitting, and sat on the edge to his side.

"Put your palm on my shoulder, Nathaniel," she said, nodding to the shoulder she meant.

"Nate, call me Nate."

With a small smile, he nodded his agreement. Daisy carefully and gently began the process of setting his shoulder back in place, and he winced as the pain washed over him.

"All right, Nate. I want you to relax your shoulder and make your arm as floppy as you can."

Nate had dislocated his left shoulder and had the palm of that arm on his lap. She had one of her hands cupping his elbow and the other was massaging the injured shoulder. She pressed her fingers to rub and cajole the shoulder so she could see which way he'd dislocated it.

His eyes never left hers. She could feel his stare, and his gaze became more intense when she glanced at him.

"Make it quick, and it will be fine."

"This will take four minutes of manipulation, but it may hurt until it's back in. Quick enough?"

"I guess. Will you talk to me while you do it?"

She deepened her voice and slowed her words as she spoke next.

"I'll use soothing sounds to lull you into thinking this is a walk in the park."

"I could listen to your voice all day long," Nate said.

She didn't look at him, instead concentrating on his shoulder, using her thumb over his shoulder and down to his upper bicep. Back and forth until she'd manipulated it back into place.

"There, you're set. It will be sore for a few days. It might be worth taking some painkillers and making sure you rest it. You don't want it popping back out."

As Daisy stood and stepped away, he lightly touched her wrist. The warmth of their skin seemed to consume her. Nate gazed into her eyes.

"Thank you," he whispered, taking a deep breath.

"Anytime," Daisy whispered back with a slight smile before turning to walk away.

"I think I broke my wrist, too," he blurted.

"What?"

"Yeah, it's looking a bit swollen," he said, nodding to the offending wrist.

Daisy looked closely, and it was red and angry.

"I have a job this evening and first thing in the morning," Nate confessed.

Feeling responsible, she went into Miss Fix-It mode. "What's the job? I might be able to help?"

He laughed, a belly laugh this time, and it irritated her. She'd spent her entire working life being laughed at. Just because she was a woman in a man's world.

"Why are you laughing? What job is it you think I couldn't possibly do? People have laughed me at my whole life from every corner, so don't piss me off, Nathaniel Hill, especially after what I just did for you."

Nate paced towards her and cupped her cheek with the hand on his sore arm. He didn't flinch even though it had to be sore.

"I'm sorry, Daisy, it's just I really don't think you can help me," he whispered.

"Try me," she said, hoping it was something she could do.

"All right, follow me," he said and took off around the side of the workshop. Daisy picked up her skirt and jogged after him. When she turned the corner, she grinned.

She was going to enjoy this.

"I need you to take those boxes out of the wheelbarrow and put them on the forklift. Then you need to drive it to the boat at the end of the quay. I was going to take them when I barrelled into you."

"Keys," she said, holding out her hand.

"You cannot drive that. You need to be trained and have certificates."

"Where are the keys, Nate?" she repeated more firmly.

"They're in the ignition," he replied.

She blanched that he would be so careless leaving the keys where anyone could go for a joyride, but then thought he could have been getting ready to make the trip before she interrupted him.

He gave her a smug smile like he was calling her bluff.

She hitched up her skirts again, ignoring his head tilt as he checked out her legs and marched to the forklift truck. She grabbed the handle above the open door and hopped in. It started as soon as she turned the key, and she drove it to the stack of three boxes that were next to the trailer. Daisy piled them on and then expertly lifted them. She swung the forklift truck around and drove to where Nate stood, opened-mouthed.

"Where is the boat?" she snapped, her eyes searching intently.

Just then, realisation dawned, and his eyes went wide.

"Fuck me, you're Daisy Turner, the one who was a total nerd in school," he said, a hint of amusement in his voice.

"Where is the boat, Nathaniel?" Daisy asked, ignoring his comment.

"Just past the warehouse Erica is setting up her charity business," he replied.

"Be right back," Daisy said, not wasting any time.

She spun around and sped off, her mind already turning to the task ahead.

Her blood ran cold as she sped down the quayside to a moored boat. She dumped the boxes, waited for the guys to pick them up and zoomed back to Nathaniel's workshop. She had forgotten about her school bully's nicknames.

Was that another thing she'd suppressed? The taunts at school because she studied hard? She only studied hard because she was lonely. Her aunt wouldn't let her have friends, and her mother was too far away to make sure she played with the other kids after school. Aunt Cynthia demanded she came home straight from school, with no exceptions. Her aunt wouldn't allow her friends to come to the estate. So she hit the books so that as soon as she was old enough, she could get the hell off Copper Island and join her brothers and father on the rigs.

When Daisy returned, she parked up the forklift around the side and found Nate lounging on the mustard armchair, cradling his elbow.

"Here are the keys to the forklift. You should never leave them in the ignition."

Daisy was so angry and disappointed that the man that made her feel human was a spiteful brat. She tossed the keys onto the counter and turned to walk away.

"I'm sorry I underestimated you. If I'd known you were Daisy Turner..."

He didn't finish, and she walked away, holding back the tears of disappointment. It was ridiculous she felt this attached to a voice, then a rumbly laugh and then his thick biceps and quick wit.

The sky was dark, with a few stars in the sky, the moon was not yet high, and it was not yet quite night. The smell of good food lingered in the air, reminding her she wanted fish and chips.

Daisy heard the crash from the shutters coming down and then running footsteps behind her. The soft thud of his footsteps was hurrying to keep up with her. When he caught up with her, she tugged her skirts loose and folded her arms across her chest as she walked, hopefully giving him clear piss-off signs.

Daisy kept walking, her feet moving faster despite her wanting to stay angry. The crunch of gravel beneath his shoes echoed louder and closer until he was beside her.

"Hey, Daisy, it's dark. I'm walking you home."

Daisy stopped walking and looked at him. He had a serious expression on his face, and his posture was stiff with determination. She hesitated for a moment before answering him.

"There is really no need. No one wants to talk to me, let alone attack me. I'm sure I'll be safe," she said evenly, not wanting to give in to her emotions.

He put up both hands in surrender as if he knew she would deny him the chance to apologise properly for his words earlier this evening.

"It doesn't matter who wants to talk or attack you. You can trust me when I say that no one will get close enough if I am by your side. Please let me do this for you? Just so you know, you are safe. That much should be my right, after all...What do you say?" His voice softened slightly as he finished speaking, giving Daisy something of an out from the conversation if she wanted it but still making it clear he wanted to walk her home and make sure she was safe from any potential danger lurking in the shadows of this island.

Daisy gave a small nod but kept walking, saying nothing else in response.

Nate ran a few steps in front of her blocking her path. He put one hand on her shoulder to stop her from running away.

"Look at me, Daisy," he said.

Daisy raised her chin and narrowed her eyes at him. He looked broody and threatening in the darkness, yet she wasn't afraid. If anything, she still wanted to wrap her arms around him and sob into his chest.

Why did he have to be him?

"What I did while we were in school was childish. I'm sorry you lost your dad. I'm sorry for a lot of things. I'm in no position to take the upper hand here. The truth is I need your help for the next few days with my forklift jobs. They're early morning and late in the evening for the next five days. Will you help me?"

Daisy looked off to the right out into the dark water. She felt so stubborn about making a truce, but it was her fault he was injured, so she needed to balance the scales.

"On one condition."

"Name it."

Daisy, a talented but awkward when she was a young girl, had been an outcast since she was a child. They ridiculed Daisy and often labelled her as nerdy or weird. It was something she had grown to loathe.

"Never call me nerdy again or Nerdy Girl," she said firmly to Nate, her voice tight with emotion. "I will not explain why, but it's important, okay?"

Nate, taken aback by Daisy's sudden outburst, nodded uncertainly. "All right," he said warily. "I'll call you Daisy."

"Thank you," she mumbled, dropping her head.

Daisy felt the weight of her anxiety lift from her shoulders, but a flood of memories quickly replaced it. She could hardly sift through them fast enough to make sense of them. The barrage of images was like a bright flickering light in her face. She winced and shied away for a few moments, trying to collect herself.

"Daisy," she heard call to her in the far distance.

She was lost in a tumult of images, each like a jagged piece of her self-image. She couldn't work out who was calling her name, just image after image of angry faces and her tears. As the chaos raged in her mind, she seemed to curl further in on herself.

Then, when soft lips touched hers, her whole mind seemed to slow to an almost stop. Her body responded to the kiss, pressing her lips to the warmth and sighing as arms wrapped around her. Soft kisses kept coming, but nothing more passionate, just reassuring caresses.

It took a few more moments for her to realise where she was and what she was doing. Finally, she opened her eyes to see a man with eyes as grey as storm clouds gazing down at her. The tenderness in his face pulled her out of her own inner turmoil, and she found herself oddly comforted by his presence.

Nate held her close, stroking her hair gently as he spoke. "I'm sorry, I didn't know what else to do to comfort you. You were shaking but couldn't hear me. It was like watching someone's heart break, and I felt the need to show you some comfort."

She nodded against his chest, grateful for the understanding she found there.

"It worked," she whispered. "Your touch made it all quiet."

"Where is the noise coming from?" he asked softly.

She shook her head and let out a sob.

"I don't know," she said helplessly. "I don't know why these images keep coming and why I can't get away from them."

She felt him nod in understanding and hold her closer, taking some of her pain away with every stroke of his hand on her back.

"Shh," he soothed, pressing kisses into her hairline. "It's okay. I'm here."

His voice was like a balm on her troubled soul, and slowly but surely, the images faded away until only their embrace remained in the darkness of its wake.

Nate wrapped his arms around her tighter, and she didn't resist inhaling motor oil and something else. Working on the rigs, oil was a comforting smell, familiar. She hadn't worked with her dad for long when he died, but she stayed on the rigs with her brothers long after. Oil mixed in with man was all she knew as familiar and comforting, and there it was in a six-foot-one man who hugged like a dream.

"It will come out bit by bit," he said soothingly. "Let me walk you home, so I know you're safe."

"Okay," Daisy said. "I came to get fish and chips."

Nate gave a rumbly laugh, and she felt it against her cheek.

"We can collect some on the way. Did you walk or come in the buggy?"

"How do you know about the buggies?"

"Archer has been back for a while. But it's Maggie that has us all laughing. She loves her buggy and has it all bling'd out. She comes zooming down this side of the quay like she's a rally driver coming to see Erica in the warehouse."

"That does not sound like Maggie, but I really want to see that," she said, grinning. "I walked."

"Okay, let's get to the chippy before it closes and then up to Turner Hall."

"I don't live there."

He frowned down at her. "Where do you live?"

"In a little cottage on the estate."

With a firm nod he said, "Lead the way Daisy."

6

Nate

Nate and Daisy arrived at the chippy at the end of the quay just in time for the last orders. He was still confused about the names she forbade him to use.

He paid attention because the vibe she carried meant there was a deep-rooted reason why.

The chippy was a small, white building with tables and benches set up outside so that customers could eat their chips while taking in views of the sea. Nate loved the place.

As they approached, Nate saw a figure clearing the tables outside, wiping the plastic surfaces and gathering the condiments to take inside. Nate casually glanced around before locking eyes with a couple, sitting at a wooden pub-style bench with plates of various fried foods.

"It looks like we're in time for last orders. What do you want?" Nate asked Daisy, who was looking anywhere but at him.

She seemed transfixed by the couple, and Nate could tell

the sight of them had stirred something deep within her. He knew this kind of concentration, and he knew the only way to find out what was really bothering her was to stay and find out.

The couple were an older couple, perhaps in their late 50s, and although they had obviously been there for some time, Nate noticed they hadn't made a move to leave. Instead, they seemed content to sit side by side, eating their chips silently. As they watched, the woman reached out and touched the man's hand gently before smiling warmly at him. They were settled. And he longed for that feeling.

Nate stood at the chip shop counter, doing his best to ignore the smell of old fat that hung in the air. He glanced over to Daisy who was standing next to him, her face hidden by her long chestnut hair. She stared out the window, her brown eyes darting to the side as if looking for something or someone.

"Daisy?" Nate prompted.

"Oh, um, I'll have chips in a cone. I can eat as I walk back home," Daisy said.

Nate gave her a pointed stare. "When *we* walk back home," he corrected.

Without another word, he put the order in for two cones of chips and a battered sausage.

"We can share the sausage," Nate said, still looking at Daisy.

She nodded, her eyes meeting his. Nate couldn't help but notice the flicker of emotion that crossed her face before she looked away. Nate knew that look. He had seen it many times before. It was the same look he saw in his own reflection in the mirror each morning.

The server handed them the food through the small service window, and the two turned and started walking.

Daisy was eating the chips from her cone, and Nate had the battered sausage balanced on top. One hand held his stack of chips. They walked together in comfortable silence, Nate not knowing what she was thinking.

"Why don't you live at Turner Hall?" Nate asked, breaking the silence as Daisy guided him up the private road to the Turner estate.

She balled up her cone and shoved it in her pocket. Nate guessed she was stalling.

The trees were thick, blocking out what was beyond them. A forest hid the estate, but as they approached, the forest thinned until it became visible through the trees.

"You don't have to tell me," he said eventually.

Daisy crossed her arms over her chest.

"I don't really know specifically, but I know I hate being in that building. Ridiculous, right? It's just bricks and mortar, but I cannot stand going beyond the kitchens in the basement."

Nate thought about saying something, but he didn't know what would be helpful or what would make things worse. He kept his mouth shut, so he tried to change the subject.

"If it gives the same reaction as I saw twice this evening, then it isn't ridiculous," he said.

Nate stared at Daisy. He had so many questions but didn't know which would be the right one to ask.

Finally, he settled on something simple.

"Do you remember why you can't stand it?"

Daisy took a deep breath and exhaled slowly.

"I remember bits and pieces," she said slowly. "It's all foggy in my head, but I remember feeling scared and alone in the dark, like I'd been abandoned."

She shuddered slightly, and Nate felt the urge to wrap his arms around her to offer comfort.

"I've told no one about this," she continued. "But I'm pretty sure that whatever happened there when I was young is why I can't stand being near Turner Hall now."

Nate nodded in understanding before reaching out and taking her hand in his own. They walked the rest of the way up the road in silence until they reached the entrance gates of Turner Hall. Daisy stopped and stared for a moment before turning away with tears in her eyes.

Nate gave her hand a reassuring squeeze as he silently vowed to protect her from whatever haunted her memories of the place.

"I'm okay from here."

He didn't doubt it, but he still wanted to walk her to her door.

Instead, he said, "Okay." Then watched her walk into the darkness of Turner Hall shadows.

7

Daisy

The following morning at six, Daisy was waiting outside his workshop for him to arrive. She didn't know what the morning's work was. Otherwise, she wouldn't have hung around and would've got to work. He had taken her at her word and taken the forklift's keys with him. Added to that, she didn't know where the crates were or the boat she needed to get them to.

"Wow, you turned up," Nate said, but she couldn't see him along the quayside.

"Up here," he said.

Daisy looked up and to the left of the workshop, and she saw Nate bare-chested with his wrist in a makeshift sling.

"You said six sharp, and here I am. What's the job?"

"There's a boat coming in at six-twenty where you dropped off the crates last night. It will probably take four runs, but the boat will have boxes for your sister-in-law's warehouse. Donations apparently she gets once a month."

"Right. Where are the keys?"

"Can you catch?"

Daisy rolled her eyes and stood from the large black mooring bollard on the side of the quay. The smooth curve was perfect for her perch until he woke up.

She sauntered over to where he was leaning out of the window and lifted her skirts out to act as a canopy to catch the keys.

"That's cheating," he said and tossed them down.

"I think the word you're looking for is practical. Do try to remember I worked on the rigs for years."

"Yes, ma'am."

She took the keys, hurried off to do his job and then by the time she returned, the workshop was open, and she could put the keys on the side table. She didn't hang around because she needed to get back up to Edward Hall.

On the fifth evening, she had left the office, jogged to her cottage, taken a quick shower, and spent too long deciding what to wear before she took the buggy down to the quayside to Hill's Workshop. Nate had badly sprained his wrist, and she felt awful as he couldn't work on any boats one-handed. At least it wasn't broken.

Thankfully the last of the forklift work was that evening, and then she was off the hook.

Daisy pulled up at the side of the workshop and switched off the engine. It was too dark to check her reflection, so she had to hope the breeze on the way down hadn't destroyed her carefully styled hair.

She picked up the carry bag of food Jason had given her and wandered around to the front of the workshop. Nate was trying to get his t-shirt off one-handed in the middle of the empty space.

"What are you doing?" she clipped out, striding towards him.

"Trying to get this shirt off. I stink and haven't showered in days since they have put this tight as fuck bandage on."

"How have you washed?"

"A bird bath each morning and night, but I'm getting pissed off and irrationally angry."

She laughed.

"I thought that was my speciality. Good to know there is someone else out there that gets stupidly angry at tiny things. Why don't you have a bath?"

"I don't have a bath, Princess," he said, giving her a grin with no heat in his words.

"I am far from a princess," she said, yanking down the t-shirt he was still trying to pull off.

"You've wanted for nothing your whole life. What does that make you?"

"Someone you do not know. You know nothing about my life, my past, my family. So stop being a jerk and making assumptions. I've had that too much for me to take it from you."

Nate looked down at her, softening his features and then sighing heavily.

"I don't think I've ever had a bath as an adult," he muttered.

"Really? Baths are the best."

"Do you have one?"

"Yes, in my cottage."

Nate kept staring at her, and she gulped a hard swallow.

Was he asking for an invitation?

It was Friday evening, and she was planning on having a bath when she was done warming his dinner like she'd done all week and making sure his side work was done.

Nate confessed on day two that he didn't have any boat work booked in, so he only needed help to ferry the crates.

"I need to get the crates done. I'll be back in half an hour. I'll put the food and my bag over on the counter. Try not to get into any trouble while I'm gone."

Nate nodded, dropped his t-shirt, and went to investigate the food while she hightailed it out of there before offering him to return to her cottage for a bath.

It only took twenty minutes to ferry the crates, and she was coming back into the workshop when someone followed her in.

"Hey, dude, you coming for a beer?" the man called out.

Daisy turned to the doorway where a good-looking, dark-haired guy about her age sauntered in. He took one look at Daisy and gave her a slow look up and down.

"Sorry, man," he said to Nate, who was scowling in the corner on his office chair. "I didn't know you had company. Who are you? I've never seen you on the island before, and it's not tourist season."

"You may not know who I am, Robert, but I know who you are," she said with such a twisted face she felt like she was emanating Cynthia Turner.

"What did I do to you? We haven't even met because, babe, I would definitely remember, no matter how drunk I was when I stuck my tongue down your throat."

Daisy hummed, twisting at the waist to look at Nate. He was wincing with his hand over his eyes.

"Have some manners, Rob," Nate said.

"I'm not the one who hasn't introduced myself. She clearly knows who I am, remembers me well it seems," he said, his grin bordering on a leer.

Robert sauntered closer, bouncing on his toes as he neared. She took a step back, and he kept coming, not reading the signals she didn't want him near her. He had the same look in his eyes many men had before when they thought they were god's gift and she should be grateful to be in their presence.

"Stay put, Robert," she said.

"Why? We've obviously been closer than this if you remember me."

She backed up again only to bump into Nate's hard body and heard him whine. She must have knocked his wrist.

"Oh yeah, dude, how's the wrist? Selly feels bad that he did that."

Even with her back to him, she knew he was shaking his head. His body had gone stiff, and she felt the draught from him, letting out a breath.

"Who is Selly?" Daisy asked softly.

Her innocent question worked, or Robert was still as stupid as he was in school. Not much had changed since she last saw him. He was just older.

"Sam Sellman, he's one of the rowers on our team. Whacked Nate here good and proper with an oar on Sunday night. You should have heard Nate howl like a baby."

Robert howled with laughter as Nate rested his good hand on Daisy's hip.

She let him.

"It's sprained, Rob," Nate said.

"No shit?"

"Yep. So no, I'm not going for a beer. I'm on heavy-duty painkillers."

"That's shit. Doesn't explain why she's here," Rob said, thumbing towards Daisy.

She internally fought the urge to kick Nate in the shin for lying and punch Rob for his disrespect. Why Nate spent any time with Rob was a mystery.

Daisy moved out of Nate's grasp to move away.

"I'm not here any more. My commitment is over. Goodbye, Nate," Daisy said.

"Ooo, what's got your knickers in a twist?" Rob said.

"Fucking hell, Rob. Leave it. Don't make things worse," Nate said.

"Worse? I still don't know who the chick is," Rob said.

She watched out the corner of her eye. Rob followed her movements around the space as she collected the dinner she'd brought for Nate and her bag from the floor. Nate wasn't going to have the homemade food after lying to her.

With her belongings, Daisy stood next to the tatty mustard armchair, watching them. Rob glanced Nate's way, and Nate was looking balefully at the food she was removing from his grasp.

"I'm Daisy Turner, and you're still the arse you were at school," Daisy said and shouldered her handbag higher up her arm.

Thankfully, he stayed where he was, thinking through was must be his mental roller-dex of school friends.

"You're Nerdy Girl?" Rob exclaimed.

Daisy stopped in her tracks and held out her hand to the nearest object to steady her dizzy body. Unfortunately, it was the mustard armchair. She glanced at it and dropped the food at her feet. Someone shouted and then wrapped their arms around her body and lifted her a few feet onto a warm lap.

"You're okay, Daisy, keep breathing," the low rumbly voice said.

She could feel trembles rocking her body, and her eyes stayed closed. A hand cupped the back of her head and guided it to a warm neck, and she cuddled in like she'd done it a hundred times. A hand smoothed her hair from her face, but the trembles were still there as the flashing images zipped behind her eyelids. When warm lips touched hers, she stilled after a few beats. Then the mouth left her, and she sagged against the warm body. Slowly after minutes, she didn't know how many, she opened her eyes. From her position, she saw the open workshop doors and the dark-as-night sky and port waters.

"Why do my feet hurt?" she muttered, looking down at her feet.

She had put on open sandals, and now food had coated her feet, and the exposed skin had turned red.

"How hot was the food when you brought it here?"

"Piping hot, the dish came straight out of the oven before I brought it here."

"Well, most of it is on the floor, but it looks like some went over your feet. It smells delicious whatever it is."

"Beef casserole. Or it was."

"You should get your feet in cold water."

"Okay," she said. "Where did Rob go?"

"I sent him away," Nate said through gritted teeth. "Rob's harmless but doesn't know where to draw the line."

"He never did. He was the one I hated most at school."

He reared his head back. "More than me?"

"Way more than you. He wasn't very nice to me."

"What did he do?"

"I'm not entirely sure."

"What do you mean?"

Daisy didn't want to confess she didn't know because she had suppressed memories coming back to haunt her. She clambered off his lap and moved to where her black leather handbag was on the floor. It was splattered with the beef casserole. Daisy brushed off as much as she could and swung it over her shoulder.

"Don't think I haven't forgotten you lied to me," Daisy said and hobbled away.

Nate was at her side in a few strides. "What do you mean?"

"You let me believe I had sprained your wrist."

"You did dislocate my shoulder," he said.

She stopped in the middle of the concrete between the workshop and the dark waters.

Her fury bubbled up, and she stabbed a finger at his chest.

"Technically, you did that when you were protecting falling on your sprained wrist. Twist it all you want, but I felt bad. I've helped around here, done your side job so you get paid, brought you meals, and you never said a word that you'd already hurt your wrist."

He moved forward, and she stepped back. He respected the move and didn't stayed still.

"Daisy, I'm sorry," he said.

"I don't care," she snapped. "Have a nice life. I thought you'd changed, thought you were a decent guy."

His retort was quick. "I am a decent guy. I am not letting you walk home after the episode you just had."

"I brought the buggy. I'll be fine," she wailed, frustrated that he thought she was helpless.

"I am not taking that chance. You don't know what you're like when you're triggered. I don't want you driving off the side of the cliff and plunging to your death."

"Why do you even care?" she yelled.

"I don't know, Daisy," he yelled back. "Maybe I like you, maybe I have this urge to take care of you, to make sure you're all right. To chase away these demons that plague you," he shouted louder. "All I know is these past five days have been the happiest days I've had in years."

"Nate," she said and sagged her shoulders.

"Don't *Nate* me. Give me a minute to lock up, and I'll chaperone you home. I can't drive."

"I'm not sure I can drive either. My feet really hurt," she muttered.

Nate let out a bark of a laugh. "What a fucking pair we make. I have feet. You have hands. You'll have to sit on my lap. I'll press the pedals, and you can steer, but I am making sure you get home safely. You can chew me out the entire way back that I let you think you'd hurt my wrist."

"Fine," Daisy conceded.

Nate grinned.

He locked up using his remote to bring the shutters down and then joined her at the buggy. She stood at the side, chewing on her thumb, wondering how it would work.

"Do those bench seats move?" Nate asked, standing next to her.

"No, they're fixed to the floor."

"Well, you're going to have to sit on my lap and drive while telling me which peddles to press as I won't be able to see past you."

"Shouldn't I just walk or get one of my brothers to come down here and get me?"

"This is my fault, and I am going to get you home. Let's move," he said, shooing her with his hands.

Daisy dropped her head back and walked to the driver's side of the buggy. Nate swung in and widened his thighs, making sure he could press the go pedal and brake pedal. Once he was happy, he patted the space between his thighs. Daisy looked doubtful she would fit, but his *hurry the fuck up* look got her hobbling over to him. She used the steering wheel to hoist her body in, and then Nate took over, holding her waist the one arm until she settled.

"My bottom is too wide for the space. I'll have to sit on you," she said.

She was ten kinds of embarrassed that she had to sit on his lap. Her skirts were thin, and there was no mistaking the warmth of his legs under her. It was a tight squeeze with her legs under the steering wheel, so she had to drape her legs over his. Nate tightened his arm and brought her back to his chest, and clung on.

"Drive us home, Miss Daisy," Nate said with an awful Southern accent.

"Oh boy, this will be the longest trip up the cliff," she muttered as she turned the ignition. "Press go but keep it easy," she said.

She reversed and then circled wide to drive along the quayside and then up the private road to the estate. She sped past Turner Hall, which was in darkness.

"I've never been up here before last week. The place looks menacing," he said.

"Trust me, it is," she replied over her shoulder. "Slow down a bit. The path is narrow as we pass Edward Hall."

"This isn't the way we walked when I brought you home last time."

"No, we came the beach pathway that time and then across the lawns. There are many ways you can get up to the estate. I use those two unless I'm heading out to see Dad's grave."

"Right," he said and tightened his hold.

She drove them in silence past Edward Hall, which had its porch light on. From the rear, they could hear generators and see spotlights. As she zipped past, there were the ends of articulated lorries.

"What's going on there?"

"They're getting it ready. A movie is shooting here in a

couple of weeks. Erica is starring in it, part of the deal of her not working away from her newborn for the first year."

"Perks of a Hollywood actress."

"There has to be some balance with the intrusion she gets. I couldn't cope with what she had to put up with. Far too private."

"That's a Turner trait," Nate commented.

"Possibly. Slow down. We're nearly there. I'm going to pull up alongside the other buggies."

Daisy counted three others, one for each of the cottages. No one lived in the fifth cottage, but there was space for a buggy if someone moved in. Daisy harboured thoughts it would be her mother, but she had a long way to go to persuade her brothers that their mother was a good person in a dangerous situation.

"Okay, we're here. I'm going to shuffle out," she said once the ignition was off.

"That's not your cottage," Nate said, nodding to Archer and Erica's place.

All their lights were out.

"That's Archer, Erica and Isobel's home. Mine is the fourth one down."

He craned his neck to see into the darkness. "Can't we get any nearer?"

"No, this is where the buggy track ends."

"What about your feet? These cottages are huge. We have at least another few minutes until we get there."

"We?"

"Yeah, Daisy. I'm walking you to your door so you get home safely."

"How will you get back?"

"My legs are fine. I'll walk back."

"All right, well, let me take these sandals off, maybe the swelling is causing the pain on the straps."

Daisy sat on the back bench facing out of the buggy and pulled on the strap to unbuckle it. She wailed at the pain and then sagged with relief when the buckle opened. Her feet seemed to swell more once she'd removed her shoes.

She gingerly stepped off the buggy and moved to the side where Nate was still sitting in the driver's seat.

"Okay, I can hobble just fine," she said.

"I could carry you?" Nate said.

"Not after a dislocated shoulder, and a sprained wrist."

"Good point. What about a piggyback?"

Daisy eyed up the distance, then looked to Jason's cottage, which was also in darkness and decided it might be her only option.

"All right," she said.

Nate grinned, moved off the seat, and then into a crouching position, putting his bad wrist in front of him and his good arm out to catch her. She gazed at his back and then at his face looking at her over his shoulder, and moved forward. She put one hand on his good shoulder and then hopped up. He caught her with his good arm and cradled her backside in his hand to shift her up his back. When she wrapped her legs around his waist, she managed to lock her ankles.

"My, my, it's like being a giraffe up here. I can see so much. Is this what it's like to be super tall. Does it snow up here in the winter?" she said, placing her hands on his head to sit up higher.

He rewarded her comments with a tap on her bottom with his fingers as she bounced along. A giggle erupted as she squinted to see as much as she could in the night. Luke's place was in darkness too, but then so was her place. They could all have been at the pub for all she knew, but then they would've invited her.

"Shit," she said and tapped his shoulder.

"Is that command to make me stop?" he said incredulously.

"Yeah. I left my handbag in the buggy. We need to go back."

"We're nearly there. Why don't I take you around the back, sit you on the armchair and then I can go back and get it."

"All right. Sounds ridiculously sensible. I quite like it up here," she said, keeping as much pout in her voice as she could.

Nate chuckled as he took the side path to her cottage, placed her on the back patio furniture, and then dashed off. She laughed for a moment and then turned solemn when it dawned on her why they were in this predicament. Her feet were scalded from her episode, and she had no way to control them. Nate had lied to her about spraining his wrist, making her feel foolish for helping him. But most of all, she couldn't get out of her head his kiss settled her, and she couldn't remember how it felt because she was out of it in an internal panic.

"Hey," Nate said, coming to a stop in front of her. He was on his knees, cupping her cheek while he checked her over. "I was gone for like three minutes."

"I'm okay, spacing out, just realised that I dropped the dinner over my feet because there is something buried deep in my head, and I'm not sane enough to work it out."

"Hey, Daisy, you're not alone in this. So many people have PTSD for all kinds of things. Stop beating yourself up. It will come out when you're ready. The fact that you're having these flashes says you are getting ready to let it out."

"You sound like you know what you're talking about."

"I read a lot," he answered.

It wasn't an answer. Did he have personal experience? She considered her next move.

"Are you still hungry?" she asked.

"I'm starving."

"Still want a bath?"

Nate grinned. "Yeah, I'd love a bath."

"All right. Let's go inside. I'll run you a bath, then I'll make us some supper."

"What about your feet?"

"I'll soak them in cold water to get the swelling down and then put on fluffy slippers and slide around the kitchen."

"You could soak your feet while I have a bath, and then we can both make supper."

"Okay," she said and nodded.

"Are you sure you're okay? You don't need a kiss to calm you or anything?"

She laughed and tapped his cheek. "You're cheeky. I don't remember your kisses, so I don't know if they're any good, but it seems I only need them when I'm spaced out."

"Is that the only time you're going to let me kiss you?"

She stilled for a moment, taking in a breath. She wanted to feel how he kissed, but there were so many reasons why that was a bad idea.

"Yeah, Nate. I'm not girlfriend material. I'm a Turner, and you don't like the Turners. I could list the rest of the reasons we should not be kissing, but it's late, and I need food and a cold compress on my feet."

Nate gave her a look that screamed she was a big hairy liar, but she didn't care. He made his feelings clear on the helpline call, so there was no point thinking they could be more than friends. She didn't think she could be friends with him, no matter how gorgeous he was. But for some reason, fate had thrown them together. She didn't hate the idea. Her reason for seeing him would be over once he left her home that evening. Daisy wondered how she would feel in the morning.

Daisy led him up the stairs, flipping light switches as she went and entered the bathroom in the main hallway. He could use that one while she used her ensuite. He was close behind her. She could feel him. It consumed her thoughts as she fumbled with the taps. To her horror, they weren't working. She twisted around, trying to lessen the number of steps she took.

Daisy looked at Nate.

He was staring at her.

She was expecting to catch him looking at her arse, but he was looking at her face, checking her features as his eyes moved about.

"What's wrong?" he asked.

"No water," Daisy said.

"Damn. I was really looking forward to a soak," he said.

Nate sifted his fingers with his good hand through his hair and down to his nape, clasping at his neck. Daisy melted at his obvious disappointment.

"Come on, there's another bathroom. I know those taps are working," she said.

Again she led the way against her better judgement. She was inviting him into her personal space. She flipped the switch on in her bedroom and did a cursory glance to make sure she had left nothing lying around. She knew she hadn't, but that was her way, triple-check everything.

"This is a nice room," Nate said, looking around.

"The cottages were designed so long ago that they positioned them to get the most of the morning and evening sun. Sunrises are spectacular from the bed. I'm looking forward to keeping the curtains open in the deepest winter so when I wake up, I'll look out and see the frost-covered lawn in the morning sun."

"Did you have that at Turner Hall? The view, I mean."

"I don't remember, really. I don't think I had romantic ideals back then. Growing up, lazing in bed and watching the sun rise was not permitted.

Sadness overwhelmed Daisy, and she stilled for a few seconds and then vigorously shook her head to try to bury the memories she wished were gone. Moving slowly across the carpeted floor, she tugged the end of her duvet so the effect was flawless on her bed and moved to the bathroom.

"Let me fill a bowl for my feet, and then I'll start the bath," Daisy said with her back turned to Nate to root around in the bottom of her store cupboard in the bathroom. She had it filled with towels of all sizes. Then she had shelves of beauty products to last years because she was still in the habit of buying in bulk, not knowing when the next delivery would come for the rigs. At the very bottom was her bowl.

"That's not a bowl, Daisy. What the fuck is it?" Nate said, stepping forward as she carried it to the bathroom and her bedroom threshold. "It has a plug."

"It's a foot spa," Daisy said defensively.

"Oh, I'm not judging. I'm a little curious and a little envious," he said.

"It's the best thing for sore feet. I'm hoping the cool water will help with the tops of my feet."

She realised she needed to fill it up, put it in the well of the free-standing bath, and turned on the cold tap. She filled it up and hobbled back to the threshold. Nate was dancing around her as she moved, so he didn't hinder her progress. All the while with a smile on his face.

"Actually, I don't need to be in here at all. I can do this somewhere else while you bathe. I don't know why I'm setting up here," Daisy said, looking around.

For some reason, she thought she'd need to babysit him, but it wasn't like he was a child.

"I'd like the company," he whispered.

Surprised at his words, she nodded.

"All right," she said and went back into her bedroom. She dragged the stool across the carpet from her vanity table, sat it at the doorway, and then plugged in the foot spa in the nearest socket. It was close enough that she could sit comfortably.

Nate had started the bath and was looking at the water when she came back in.

"Do you want bubbles or just warm water?" she asked.

"I want the full works, whatever you'd have," he said, looking at her in wonder and then her cupboard of delights.

"Bubbles it is. I have red, blue or purple."

"Blue," he said immediately.

"They're on the middle shelf. Help yourself. I'm going to leave you alone while you undress and get into the bath. When you're submerged, give me a yell, and I'll come back and keep you company."

"Umm," Nate said.

"What now?" she huffed out.

He gave her a lopsided grin. "I need some help to undress."

"This is day five. What have you been doing until now?"

"Well, the jeans and boxers are okay. They drop to the floor as soon as they are over my hips, but the t-shirt is a problem. I've cut them off."

"You're kidding?"

"Nope. But as I need to walk home, it's too cold to do that half dressed."

Daisy sighed so loudly she thought she might growl. Undressing Nate was not part of the deal. She didn't want to see the firm chest he'd held her against. It didn't matter how attractive he was. This wasn't a man she would get intimate with.

"Turn around," she said.

Nate complied even though his face said he didn't want to. Daisy gave him a stern look, and he turned away, chuckling as he did. She pushed his t-shirt and jumper up as one, and he raised his arms, but she wasn't tall enough.

"Crap. Turn around," Daisy said.

Nate dropped his arms, and the clothing fell back in place. He turned to face her, and his eyes gazed hard. Her entire body heated in response.

"Lift your arms," she whispered. "Then bend at the waist towards me."

He silently did as she asked. Daisy stepped forward so her torso pressed against his good shoulder, and she curled her fingers around the hem of his t-shirt and jumper. She pulled as she hobbled back and took the clothing with her. She stumbled in her haste and plopped down on the side of the bath, almost falling in. When Nate stood upright, she grabbed the taps to steady herself.

He was beautiful. Smooth skin everywhere, not a blemish or a mark in sight. His muscled arms curved at the shoulder and then again at his biceps. It was no wonder she felt safe in his arms. They looked as strong as they felt. His chest was broad with slightly pronounced pecs but not too bulky. Then his nipples, erect and pebbled like he was shivering from the cold.

She'd spent so much time checking him out that she expected smugness when she looked at his face, but all she saw was vulnerability.

"I should let you get undressed and into the water while it's warm."

He gave her a stiff nod and turned his back while he undid his jeans with one hand. She hadn't dared look lower. She wouldn't know what to do with a man like Nate Hill. Scurrying out of the room, she winced and yelped as she moved across the carpet. It was her turn to undress, and she did in her walk-in wardrobe as she'd forgotten to close the bathroom door. Turning around was tempting, but she'd made a pact that she was going nowhere near Nate and his dislike for her. She pulled on shorts, a t-shirt and then tied her hair up into a bun.

"You in the bath?" she called out.

"Yeah," Nate said with a long sigh. "This is like heaven."

"Have I turned you into a bath junkie?" she asked as she approached the doorway.

Plonking her bottom down on the circled velvet stood, she placed her feet in the cold water and moaned. The cool against the heat of her feet was delicious.

She sagged as she moved her feet over the bobbled floor pressing the pressure points on her soles.

"What is in that bowl that has you moaning like a porn star?" Nate said.

She snapped her eyes open and looked at him submerged up to the chin in bubbles. Daisy narrowed her eyes.

"Did you put more bubble bath liquid in?"

"You left me unsupervised. It didn't look like you'd put enough in."

"Amateur," she muttered. "I put the perfect amount in."

"Well, I think this is perfect."

Daisy looked at his arm resting against the lip of the bath and then at his face. The bubbles were still growing, and he now had a beard. She laughed.

"We don't make a good one between us. I hope this sorts out my feet."

"Me too. I'm sorry about Rob."

"He wasn't to know. He was always an ass. You two terrorised me through school. I don't have fond memories of either of you."

"Yet here I am naked in your bathroom," he sang.

"If Luke finds out, he will go mad and hunt you down. So let's keep this between us. He was the one who found me crying when I walked home after your taunts. You all had it wrong about us Turners. Luke especially hates bullies, so don't be bragging about being here."

"I'm probably going to steer clear of all your brothers. I'm not sure any of them liked me picking on their little sister."

Daisy smiled wide. "Probably a good thing."

They sat in silence. Daisy wished she'd remember to bring her book with her.

"Can you pass me a towel? I'm getting wrinkly in here," he asked.

Daisy turned her back to Nate and counted to five. He was about to rise out of the bath with water pouring down his body like a Greek God, but she wouldn't get a glimpse. It was a bad idea to get involved with Nate in any capacity. Reaching for the towel from the cupboard, she held it out behind her back, shaking it after a second when he didn't take it.

"You're not close enough, Daisy. Come nearer."

She could hear his tease and debated if she would take

the bait. She turned around, looked at the ceiling, and lowered her eyes until she met Nate's scorching stare. Her heart stumbled for a second while she collected herself and stopped from stripping naked and joining him in the bath. Keeping her eyes locked in his, she shoved the towel at his torso. She then walked out of the bathroom to the sounds of his chuckles.

She knew her cheeks were beetroot because she could feel the heat.

8

Nate

*N*ate looked around the nurse's room, paling at the various pregnancy posters and thanked his lucky stars that he couldn't give birth. To distract him from what looked painful, he probed Heidi for information.

"So you married a Turner," Nate said as he swung his legs on the bench seat.

He was in the nurse's room at the doctor's surgery.

"I did," Heidi replied, eyeing him sceptically.

"How is it?"

"Married, or married to a Turner?" she asked, peeling back the elastic bandage from his sprained wrist.

He hadn't seen Daisy for two weeks and was desperate for a reason to see her.

"Married to a Turner."

"Why?" her scepticism was replaced with a gleeful glance. "You like Daisy?"

"Do you know her?"

"A little. She's the last of the siblings to come back to the island. She's been on the mainland for a while."

Nate watched as Heidi tested his wrist. She usually only dealt with pregnant women or new mothers, but the surgery was busy. She was on minor ailments, which included him.

"This is looking good, Nate. You don't need another bandage but don't go overboard carrying any weight for another couple of weeks."

"Okay, thanks."

"Listen, Nate. I'm not sharing about the Turners because it's their stuff to tell, but my husband and his siblings are good people. If you like Daisy and can promise you'll treat her well, I'll tell you where her office is."

"I will treat her like the diamond she is."

"Okay. She's tough and resourceful. I suspect she has had to cope on her own a lot longer than her brothers think. So watch and listen, and you'll be fine."

Heidi snapped off her gloves and threw them in the disposal.

"Where is her office?" he asked, getting off the bench and turning his wrist to test it out. The indentations of the bandage fascinated him for a few moments.

"Have you been beyond Turner Hall?"

"Yep," he said.

"Have you been beyond Edward Hall?"

"I have," he said in a conspiratorial tone.

"Have you?" she asked, stepping forward, dropping her nurse's persona and morphing straight into gossip girl. "Have you been inside her cottage?"

"Heidi, I thought we weren't sharing here?" he teased.

"Oh God, this is gold. Daisy doesn't let anyone in, metaphorically or physically. This makes me really happy. Please don't fuck this up. You were awful to her in school."

"Why has everyone got a long memory? It was a long time ago," Nate said, flinging his arms out.

"People always remember their bullies, even when they don't want to," Heidi said, her tone turning serious.

It was then it dawned on him what Daisy might have been suppressing.

"Right. Gotcha. You have my word. I have nothing but good intentions towards Daisy," he promised.

"Good. I want to see her happy."

"Office. Location," he bit out.

"Oh right, yes."

Heidi pulled a piece of paper from the photocopier and drew him a map. Grinning, he took it from her, stuffed it into his pocket and marched out of the doctor's surgery. He was a free man to hold Daisy tightly.

He was not going to let go.

9

Daisy

The redness had completely gone from her feet, but the dull ache of missing Nate remained. She was too embarrassed to go and visit his workshop, which was his home too. Thankfully she hadn't had another episode.

Daisy walked across the grass lawns. She admired the dew on the grass. It was beautiful to look at but a pain when she wore her suede shoes. Now that October had arrived, she had switched her flats to chunky leather booties for her daily trek to Edward Hall.

Teddy had waited for her at the back door of Archer's place and bounded out when he saw her walk across the grass. With a little baby in the house, Archer had fitted a dog flap, so he didn't need to get up for the baby and their dog. She'd fallen into her routine of getting up before the sun, going for a run, coming back for a shower and then dressing for work. Thicker dark-coloured skirts had replaced her boho flowy skirts. By the time she reached Archer's cottage, the hem was already sodden.

Daisy waited at the opening in the squat wall for Teddy to come running out. Archer stood in the open back door with a cup of coffee wearing PJ bottoms and a long-sleeved t-shirt. His hair was all over the place as Teddy escaped through the open door.

"I'll be over in an hour to get him for his walk," Archer said through a yawn.

"All right, you know where to find us," Daisy said, patting her thigh.

Teddy slowed his run as he approached and greeted her with a lick of her hand. She bent, scratched his head, and smoothed a hand down his spine.

"Why are you in so early? The sun is only getting above the horizon?"

"Lots to do, Archer. I prefer to start early so I can finish at a decent time. I've always been a lark."

"Hmm, I think I'm an owl in that case. See you later," Archer said, raising his mug and then closing the back door.

Daisy chuckled as she strode through the grass rather than use the flagstone path to her office. It was a much quicker route than the long way around, and she had a stack of work waiting for her. Entering Edward Hall via the kitchens, she walked through the vast space of stainless steel tables and appliances. The breakfast staff was preparing the feast for the movie set staff, who seemed to work all hours of the day and night. A lot of the crew were staying at Edward Hall.

The leading actor was staying elsewhere, she didn't know where and Erica cosied up in her cottage. The supporting actors scattered, with some staying in Edward Hall and some staying in B&Bs in town.

Many residents had spruced up their spare rooms and rented them out for the duration of the filming. Something Archer had organised through the town council as a way for the residents of Copper Island to earn an income.

With only two pubs, they were full most nights. Every eatery was full too.

She'd learned via her mum, who had got it from her parents, that the suppliers and shops in town were grateful for the custom in what would usually be a quiet month as the tourist season was over. She and her brothers had planned an event every month of the following year, so the residents could make hay when the sun shone all year round and not just in the summer months, albeit summer lasted a lot longer than the mainland because of their location.

"Hey, Sis," Jason called out as she was halfway across the kitchens.

"Hey, Jason. I haven't seen you for a few days."

He looked up from where he was leaning over the workbench, pen in hand, flipping the pages of a notebook.

Jason grinned when he spotted her.

"I've been menu planning and finding sources for the products we need. I went to the mainland on an impromptu trip for a couple of days, and I think I have a new supplier that can ship over what we need to keep the crew fed and not eat the same thing most days."

Daisy was talking and moving at the same time. She couldn't linger, or the bacon smells would get her.

"Great. I bet they'll be happy. They'll leave Copper Island spoilt."

"That's the intention. They can tell all their movie mates, and then we'll get more films being made here."

"We can only hope," Daisy called out.

"Your breakfast is on your desk," he called to her back.

"You're my favourite brother, Jason," she hollered, nearly at the internal door to the main part of Edward Hall.

"You say that to all of us," he said.

She did when she wanted something from them. Which wasn't often.

Pushing through the swing door, Daisy walked across the marble floor to the front door and let in Teddy. He knew he wasn't allowed through the kitchens, so Teddy branched off when Daisy took the shortcut.

"Come on, Teddy," she said, and he bounded in out of the damp morning and was at her side as they walked to her office, and she opened the door. On the middle of her desk was a bowl of warm porridge and a pot of honey to the side. If Jason wasn't about, one of his deputies made her breakfast and put it in a thermos flask as they weren't as familiar with her arrival time. It was sweet, and she treasured the welcome at her crack of dawn start. She set the coffee machine going before she shucked off her coat and hung it on the coat stand.

It was time for her to multitask.

She ate her porridge while reading her emails and then got to work to ensure their livelihood was still intact. She had a brief conversation with Warren, who was coming to the island soon, and before she knew it, lunchtime had arrived. It was signalled by dozens of people walking past her office floor-to-ceiling sash window. In the summer and until recently, she could push up the bottom part of the window to let in the cool breeze, but now it acted as a draught. It was a reminder she needed heavy curtains in the room if she didn't want to freeze to death.

Most of the people were passing from right to left so she could see their faces, then there was a single person going the wrong way, looking up at the building and then over his shoulder. Daisy only saw the back of his head but knew who it was. She then saw two burly men stride after him.

Daisy knew who they were too.

Security.

Why were the security guys doing chasing after Nate?

Curiosity got the better of her, and she swished the catch and pushed up the window. It was so large she could duck and be out on the ledge. It was a two-foot drop to the grass at the rear of the grounds. Daisy looked right to see Nate speed walking and looking up at the building still and the security guys following at a swift pace.

"Nate," she shouted.

All three men looked her way. Nate sagged his shoulders and threw up his hands. The first thing she noticed was there was no cast on his wrist, and second, he had shoved the sleeves of his fleece up to his elbows.

Didn't he feel the cold?

He came jogging towards her and glared at the two security guards who followed close behind.

"You know this guy?" Sid, head of security, asked.

"Yeah, he fixes boats in town. He's fine to be up here."

"All right. He seemed dodgy when he didn't know where you worked but said you'd vouch for him."

"I will," Daisy said and gave Nate a warning glare, who was warming up his smug smile.

Sid and his partner sauntered off, and Daisy jumped down into the grass and crossed her arms over her chest to keep warm.

"Why are you here?"

"I came to see you," he said and smiled.

"Why?"

"I missed you," he said.

"What?"

"Can we go inside? It's freezing out here."

"All right," Daisy said, glancing at his wrist. "You could pull down your sleeves."

Nate chuckled. He climbed up on the ledge and then dropped into her office. Daisy waited for Nate to move further in, pushed the sash window down, and fixed the latch. She was more bothered about keeping that window locked than she was about her back door.

Nate moved to the other side of the room, where her coffee machine was sitting on the sideboard.

"Can I have a coffee?" he asked.

"Sure, milk is in the fridge underneath. Can you make me one too?"

"How do you take it?"

"Just milk, a splash."

Nate set about making the coffee, and she took her seat behind her desk and closed her laptop lid to make her monitor screen go dark. It was a bunch of numbers that wouldn't make sense, but she was in the habit of always hiding her work.

Nate came over to the seat opposite her desk and placed the mugs on the desk. He made himself comfortable with his legs stretched out. His feet ended up under the desk and resting next to her feet.

She eyed him carefully, her expression giving no indication as to what she was thinking. She didn't give away if she was annoyed or amused or if she was even surprised that he was there.

"Why are you here?" she asked.

He swallowed hard, his eyes darting to the side out of the window he'd come through.

"You never sent me the list," he said.

She tilted her head slightly, her eyes narrowing in confusion.

"What list?"

"The list of reasons why I can't kiss you," he replied.

A small smile tugged at the corner of her lips. "Oh, that list. Well, it's endless. I thought my surname was enough of a deterrent."

He looked down at his shoes, his cheeks growing red.

"It wasn't," he said quietly. "You seem to think I hate all things Turner."

"I know you hate all things, Turner. You have for a long time, at least during school, and it seems you blame the Turners for the downturn in business."

She didn't want to reveal she knew who he was on the call.

"Every business owner on the island thinks that. I'm not alone in feeling the pinch. This movie seems to have got the town buzzing."

"So you don't hate the Turners?"

"No, but I still don't like what they've done to the island."

"When you say they, I am a Turner," Daisy said, exasperated.

"Not really. You haven't played a part in the last six years. You haven't been here. I didn't like you at school for different reasons."

That got her attention.

"What reasons were they?"

"You were so tight with your brothers. The four of you stuck together like glue. No one could infiltrate the bond you had except for Keith and Heidi. Then something imploded there, and then there was Freya and Luke. But no one else got in. You wouldn't give anyone the time of day like we were not good enough."

"But that wasn't true. We had a lot to deal with."

"Don't we all?" he said, reaching for his coffee.

He took a sip and then set it down again. Daisy shifted in her chair, making it squeak. That got an amused smile from Nate.

"I don't know what to say," Daisy said, looking straight at Nate.

"What else is on the list? Because it seems you like talking to me, and for some reason, I settle your soul when I kiss you. The downside is that you're so spaced out you don't get to enjoy them, so I don't know if I'm violating you somehow."

She was floored at what he'd said, so she quickly put his mind at rest. "You're not violating me, Nate. I don't know why you settle me, but you do."

"You settle me too," he murmured.

Nate took another sip of his coffee, and so did Daisy. She didn't know where to take the conversation next. Thankfully Nate did.

"Have you had any more episodes?"

"Not since the last one with Rob."

"That's good."

Silence fell between them again, and Daisy's coffee was nearly finished. She was about to ask Nate a question as he stared out of the window when the door flung open.

Stan Myers stood on the threshold. His hair was out in all directions. His bucket hat was nowhere in sight.

"Daisy," he said with a sigh, his eyes narrowing in on the back of Nate's head. "Hi, Nate."

"Hey Stan," Nate said, raising his mug but not turning around.

"How did you know it was Stan?"

"He has a unique voice."

"Oh," she said to Nate.

Daisy then looked at Stan and stared into his eyes and then groaned. "No."

"I haven't said anything," Stan whined.

"Still no, Stan. Surely Jason, Archer or Luke can help. I play with calculators. What could you need with me?"

Nate laughed at her comment and sipped from his mug.

Stan dragged out his hand from his coat pocket.

Daisy was raising her hand, palm out to Stan.

"No, Stan, put your hand back in your pocket."

"Too late," he said, bringing out the spanner.

Daisy sagged in her chair and fake cried. "It can't be my turn," she wailed.

Nate was laughing at her antics.

"Your brothers said if it's something any of you can sort out, then it's your turn."

She sighed, dropped her head into her hands and stifled a groan. She had a lot of work to get done.

"What is the issue?"

"The lead actor has a problem."

Daisy snapped her head up and gave him her squinted stare.

Nate moved his chair to the side so he could watch the proceedings like it was a tennis match.

"Can't the director or producer help?"

"It's not a movie issue."

"Then what is it?"

"He broke his boat."

Silence.

Then Daisy's eyes shot straight to Nate, and he grinned like a Cheshire cat, folding his arms across his chest and leaning back in his chair on the back legs.

"This can't be a coincidence," Daisy said low, feeling like she'd been set up.

"It kind of is but kind of isn't. See, I saw Nate skulking about when I was trying to figure out a way to sort the problem, and then I put two and two together. The actor is living on his boat while filming here, and something is wrong with something. I forget the terminology. I was busy trying to find where we could put him up while he was filming, not thinking we could fix his boat. I went to Hill's Workshop, and it was all closed up. Now I know why."

"Did you even try my brothers?" Daisy said with a sigh.

Stan stalked forward, tossed the spanner on the table and then retreated to the threshold.

"No. Can you convince Nate to fix his boat so he can stay on it and the filming won't be delayed? We want to make a good impression."

Daisy looked from Nate's smug grin to Stan's wide-mouthed eek face and back to Nate. She knew this would cost her and cost her big, but she was all for making Edward Hall a success.

"I'll give it my best shot, but Nate here hates the Turners, so I don't know if I can pull it off," Daisy said.

Nate didn't correct her, and she looked at Stan. He was shrugging his shoulders like this wasn't news to him.

"Good luck," Stan stage whispered and closed the door on them.

"Shit," Daisy said.

"I cannot wait for this," Nate said, rubbing his hands.

Daisy sighed heavily. "Name your terms."

Eight hours later, Daisy was sitting on a cushion, snuggled into a jumper five times too big for her, leaning against the bathtub in her ensuite. She'd called Archer for him to look at her guest bathroom, and he'd fixed the taps in there, but the deal was, Nate could take a bath in her bathroom with her there for company.

He had ten tokens.

She knew this because he made her design them when they were in her office and printed them out. Then he took one pen from the mug she housed them in and made her sign all ten tokens.

Nate safely nestled them in his wallet. Well, nine of them were. She'd set light to the one he'd given her straight away for that evening. Which was right then.

Nate splashed around in the bath, spraying droplets over the page she was reading. Her knees were bent with the book resting against her thighs while she clutched her oversized mug filled with tea.

"Hey, you'll get my book wet," she said, not looking around at what he was doing.

It was enough to set her skin aflame to know he was naked, inches away from her. She didn't need to look at him too. The scent of the strawberry bubble bath wafted around her. Nate spent a long time choosing which scent he was going to have for someone who hadn't taken a bath for a good amount of years.

"What are you reading?" he asked.

"A memoir from World War II," Daisy muttered, turning the page.

The deal was him having a bath with her in the room. No mention of chit-chat.

"Is it good?"

"Yeah. Copper Island Library doesn't have a massive selection, so I grabbed the first book I saw."

"Don't you have a massive library at Turner Hall?"

"Aunt Cynthia has a massive library at Turner Hall.

They're not my books, not that I would step foot in that building. Well, not the main part, anyway."

"Don't you like her?"

Shit.

She'd revealed too much.

Daisy went with honesty.

"No."

Taking the hint, Nate shuffled up to where she was at the end of the bathtub. Her head was by the taps, and his arm was touching the side of her head. She leaned against him for two seconds, then realised what she was doing and straightened.

"Will you read some to me?"

"Are you sure? It's not that exciting at the moment."

"I like hearing your voice."

This time Daisy did turn around. His head was above the lip, with peaks of bubbles all around him. He looked youthful with his damp hair and a boyish grin.

Daisy settled back, put her mug on the floor and turned the page. Nate gently put his palm on her forehead and guided her to rest against his arm.

She did as he guided, and never in all her memories had she felt so relaxed. Narrating the story wasn't as daunting as she thought it would be, and soon the pages were turning, and Nate stayed where he was with her head resting against the warmth of his arm. After an hour and Nate topping up the bath twice, she closed her book.

"I can feel my eyes drooping. I need to stop."

"Okay. Thank you for reading to me."

"You seem to be making yourself at home in my tub."

"It's a nice tub."

"Hmm. I'll leave you to get dry and dressed. I'll meet you in the kitchen."

Daisy didn't wait for his answer and stood, grabbing her cushion and empty mug. Then she had the dilemma of the book still on the floor. Nate reached forward, showing all his naked back muscles and lifted it to push it into the pouch of her oversized jumper that fell to her knees.

"Thanks," she said.

"I'm standing up in three seconds. I have no issue with you watching but fair warning."

Daisy turned on the spot and strode out of the room to the sound of Nate chuckling. Tossing the cushion on her bed, she placed the book on her nightstand she took her mug downstairs. Daisy waited for Nate to come down and join her, and they ate the cheese, meats and bread she'd laid out. He had a beer, and she had a glass of wine.

They acted as if they had known each other all their lives.

10

Nate

*A*fter nearly two weeks of trekking up to Daisy's cottage using his tokens, the security guys on the movie set knew who he was and gave him a nod when he passed them. He went the long way around to get to her via her office window in case she was still working. That had happened one evening the previous week.

The office was in darkness when he strode by, and he jogged the rest of the way to her cottage. When he got to her back door, it was open. The kitchen was in darkness, and he couldn't hear anything. The house was so eerily quiet. Still, somehow he knew Daisy was at home.

Nate bolted up the stairs knowing the layout of the cottage blindfolded, and headed straight to her bedroom. Daisy huddled in the corner on the other side of the vast room as big as his workshop. Her knees were up, she'd wrapped her arms around her shins, and she stared into space.

This was the third time he'd seen her like this, and he hated it. Not only did it scare the shit out of him, but there was so much pain distorting her face he wanted to rip the memories out of her head.

Nate fell to his knees in front of her and then flopped back on his arse with Daisy in his arms. He rocked her from side to side as she burrowed into him. He kissed her temple and then eased her back in his arms to press a kiss to her mouth. She had kissable lips, plump and soft, and he wished to fuck that she felt his kiss because he wanted her to kiss him back so badly.

"Daisy," he whispered over her lips. "Come back to me."

Her mouth twitched below his, and he kissed her again, more firmly than the last two times to see if she would come round more quickly. To his surprise, she puckered her lips and pecked at his mouth. He stayed where he was, brushing his lips over hers as she came around from her spaced-out daze. He didn't dare move until he knew she was lucid and at the moment.

"Nate, what happened?" she whispered, her voice filled with panic.

He moved back to focus on her face. Her eyes were still closed, and she whispered like she was hoarse.

"I found you in the corner, curled up, knees to chest, rocking."

"I'm not sure what triggered it."

"If a memory from years ago invades your head and scares you, it's possible you are still dealing with that fear internally, especially if it comes up without you consciously bringing it up. The memory stresses your body and reacts. In your case, it shuts down, possibly because you're not ready to deal with it. But the fact they are coming out now could mean you're strong enough to meet the fear head-on.

If you don't consciously deal with it, then your body and head are going to think you might end up in the same situation. So we need to come up with why you have these flashbacks and why you think it may happen again. Then we need to put things in place to prevent that from happening. I suspect you are already doing one of those things, but avoidance isn't acceptance."

Daisy hummed but said nothing.

"Have these been happening outside of the two times you had them with me?"

"Yeah," she said and then burst into tears.

"Hey, don't cry. You're safe here with me," he said and kissed her cheek. "You're going to be okay."

"I hate that this is happening. It's too much for my mind to process being back on Copper Island."

"Please don't say you want to move away," Nate said.

He was frantic that she might run away. Daisy had already told him she'd run away for a month after the first flashback when she saw Luke argue with one of the staff from Turner Hall. Getting to know Daisy night after night was the highlight of his day. He fixed the actor's boat in record time, so the customer had given him a list of things to do on the boat during the day while he was filming. It still gave him his evenings free.

He usually slouched on his sofa, watched TV, or went for a pint, but that all changed once he'd swam in her tub. It had nothing to do with bathing in luxury and everything to do with the bohemian woman in his arms. He never wanted to spend another day away from her.

Maybe he was being overprotective, but she needed looking after, and her brothers checked in on her but not on a deep level. She had three friends that he could tell, and they were her brothers' wives and fiancée. They led busy lives, and Nate wasn't sure she was sharing her pain with them for fear it would get back to her brothers. Daisy said they have their own pain to work through and didn't want to bother them with hers.

"Would you miss me or my bath?"

Nate grinned and pretended to think about it.

He wanted to be skin-to-skin with her and not have sex. Nate needed her to know how much she meant to him since they met a month ago.

Nate knew he couldn't let Daisy out of his sight, not even for a moment. He was afraid that she'd disappear like a gust of wind, never to be found again. Her pain was too much for her to bear alone, and he was the only one who could comfort and make her feel alive again.

"Will you have a bath with me?" Nate asked.

"Yes," she said instantly.

Nate's heart skipped a beat.

Undoubtedly, he wanted to take her to bed, but he wanted to take things slow.

Nate had long longed to hear those words, but he didn't want to take advantage of her vulnerability.

"Are you sure, Daisy? I don't want to push you into anything you're not ready for."

Daisy smiled at him, her eyes glimmering with unshed tears. "I'm sure, Nate. I trust you."

Nate knew he couldn't resist her any longer. He leaned in, lifted her up, and carried her to the bathroom. Nate sat her on the chair in the corner and stripped down to his boxers. Turning on the taps, he swiped his hand back and forth under the water for the correct temperature and then turned to Daisy.

Nate knew he couldn't let her slip through his fingers. He had never felt this way for anyone, not even his high school girlfriend, who left him and moved off the island a few years ago. Daisy was different. She was vulnerable yet strong, and he always wanted to be there for her.

As he stood there, their eyes locked in a trance. Nate could feel the chemistry between them growing stronger every second. As they stared, he couldn't resist moving across to her and tugging off her jumper.

He leaned down and pressed a kiss to her cheek. She was flush, from what he wasn't sure, as the room was filling with steam from the hot bath.

"What flavour are we going for today?"

"Strawberry," she said and stood to move to the cabinet.

Nate let her do what she needed, so she was voluntarily getting into the bath with him.

As she rummaged through the cabinet, Nate couldn't help but admire her figure. The tight-fitting tank top and leggings she was wearing accentuated her curves. He could feel his arousal growing, but he tried to suppress it. He didn't want to come on too strong and ruin the moment.

Finally, she found what she was looking for and turned to face him. In her hand was a bottle of strawberry-scented bubble bath. She walked over to the tub and poured a generous amount of the pink liquid into the warm water.

Nate watched as the bubbles formed, creating a frothy layer on the surface of the water. He took off his boxers, revealing all of his body. He stepped into the tub, feeling the warm water enveloping him. Nate didn't dare look to see if Daisy approved of how he looked. If she did, there would be no way of hiding his erection. If she didn't, he feared he might cry.

He could see from the corner of his eye Daisy removing her clothes. He couldn't look away once he moved his head.

She was hiding a fantastic figure under her clothes. Everything about her was tight and toned.

Dropping his hand into the water, he forced his arousal down by pinching the head and pushing.

"Come on in," he said, extending his hand to her. "The water's perfect."

She hesitated for a moment, then Daisy threw one leg over, and he had to shut his eyes from the vision of her perfect pussy on show. She was completely bare. He opened his eyes once he felt her legs press against his splayed knees.

The bubbles covered their bodies.

As she settled at the other end of the bath, Nate moved his hand to her ankle and lifted it so it rested on his hip. He nodded to her other leg for her to mirror the action. Nate needed her to participate.

"Are you okay?" he asked her.

Daisy nodded, her eyes wide at what she was doing. She looked terrified. He wanted to bring her closer.

Afraid he might scare her away, he stayed at his end of the tub.

But Nate wanted her on his lap, his cock deep inside her.

"If you want to get out, just get out. Don't worry about my feelings. If you want me to close my eyes when you get out, then say it. You won't offend me. I would prefer you down this end, but I get why you're at that end. I won't move. You're safe here."

"Okay," she said, looking at him.

That one word nearly killed him. Daisy seemed so inside herself, the spark lost from their sparring the night before.

"Tell me what you were doing before I found you?"

She frowned. "What do you mean?"

"To make you cower in the corner, something must have

made you feel that way. It looked to me like you were hiding, but there wasn't anyone in the cottage."

"I'd got changed out my work clothes into comfy, sitting in a bathroom, clothes," she said, her lips tipping up.

Thank God she was coming back to herself. Nate began to relax.

"Go on," he said, slouching down and putting his feet on either side of her hips.

"I'd gone to the window to close the curtains," she said.

Then she craned her neck to look out through the bathroom door into the bedroom.

"I can't see. Are the curtains closed?"

Nate turned around and saw most of the windows, then turned back.

"One is open, and one is closed."

"I must have seen something," she mused.

"Someone from the movie set?"

"I doubt they would get past the security fences erected to protect the cottages."

"You must have seen something that sent a message to your mind that scared you."

"I'm not sure what would have sent me into a spiral. Thank you for turning up when you did. I'm not sure how long it lasts."

It was on the tip of his tongue to offer to move in, but even to him that sounded extreme, but she brought out all his protective instincts. He couldn't bear the thought of her being alone in the cottage, terrified and vulnerable to whatever it was that had caused her distress.

As Nate looked at her, he couldn't help but notice how strikingly beautiful she was. Her long dark hair cascaded down her back in gentle waves, and her eyes seemed to sparkle with intelligence and humour.

He cleared his throat and tried to sound casual. "Listen, I know this might sound crazy, but why don't I come and stay with you for a few days? You have a spare room, and it might help you feel more at ease."

He couldn't explain why he felt so drawn to her, but something about her made him want to keep her safe at any cost.

She looked wary, so he changed the subject.

"Do you have anyone to talk to apart from me?"

"I talk to my mum. She's trying to help me work out what is freaking me out. I send her pictures of where I am after it happens. Did you know the armchair in your garage used to be in my playroom at Turner Hall?"

"Seriously?"

"Yeah. How did you get it?"

"My dad bought it from someone on the island. I'm not sure, really. I can ask him when I call him next."

"I think that might help. It seems bizarre that you have it."

"Maybe it is fate."

She gave him a baleful look, and he grinned.

"Daisy?"

"Yeah?"

"I didn't think any of you were in contact with your mother. Throughout school, it was rife about your mum leaving your dad and the four of you. Do your brothers talk to her too?"

Daisy shook her head and played with the bubbles that reached her chin as she dipped lower. Her calf brushed his thigh, and he wanted to yank her forward so she was on his lap and he was inside her.

"They're going to hate I've been in contact with her."

"Why?"

"Because they don't like she walked out and left us."

"She didn't walk out on you?"

"No. She had to leave. If Mum hadn't left, she would've killed her."

"Who Daisy? Who would have killed her?"

Daisy dropped her head into her hands and let out a loud sob. There was no way Nate was leaving her at the other end of the bath. He scooted forward, water slopping over the sides and scooped her up to sit sideways on his lap.

Daisy's tears continued to flow down her face as Nate held her tightly in his arms. She buried her face in his chest, her sobs muffled.

Nate stroked her hair softly, whispering sweet nothings in her ear. He couldn't bear to see her so upset and knew he had to do something to make her feel better.

"I'm not going anywhere," he said firmly, his voice gentle and soothing. "I care about you, Daisy. I'm right here."

Daisy looked up at him, her eyes red and puffy from crying. She searched his face for any sign of doubt. He hoped all she saw was sincerity.

"I care about you too. I barely know you, but I wouldn't want to be in anyone else's arms," she whispered, leaning in to kiss him.

Their lips met in a tender caress. As they kissed, the water sloshed around them, the steam rising from the surface. Nate pulled away before it got too heated.

"I really want to kiss you properly, but this seems an inappropriate time."

"This is the perfect time," she whispered, lifting her fingers to press against his lips. "At least I'll remember it this time."

Nate cupped the back of her head and took in every inch of her face. He needed to be sure she wanted him to kiss her because he knew it wouldn't be quick once he did. Nate squashed her breasts against his chest, her arse on his thigh, and his cock was telling her loud and clear he wanted her. There was nothing he could do about that. Nate would not hide his desire. He wouldn't act on it either until she was ready.

"You ready?" he asked with a grin.

"Yeah, kiss me like you want me,"

"Oh, I want you, Daisy Turner, more than you can imagine."

He leaned down and moved his head from side to side, brushing his lips across hers for a few beats until he pressed hard. On the second kiss, he swiped his tongue along her bottom lip, and then he swooped inside. She jolted in his arms at the same time he did. It was like someone had put a live wire on his heart. He knew she felt it too because she couldn't get close enough and kissed him so wildly he could barely keep pace. His aloof, distant Daisy was now passionately kissing him, dancing her tongue in and out of his mouth.

He wanted to marry her.

Right then, at that moment, he wanted Daisy as his wife.

She was the one he'd been waiting for.

To love her, protect her.

If he could wangle it, he never wanted to leave her side. The jolt of electricity, the electric kiss happening right then, was all he needed to know.

11

Daisy

Daisy sat on the stainless steel workbench, swinging her legs deliberately out of sync with Jason, knowing it would drive him mad. She smiled when she saw him try to change speed to keep in time with her, but she changed direction.

"Daisy," he huffed out.

"Free your mind, brother. You don't have to be in step with the rest of the world."

Jason turned his head slowly and looked at her.

"That's a bit deep for this time of day."

She let out a short laugh, looked at her brother, and gave him a fond smile.

"Why are you so happy?" Jason asked, narrowing his eyes.

"I'm always happy."

"Happier, then."

Daisy shrugged and looked ahead as the side door from

the outside opened, and Luke hefted in a stack of ledgers. Archer was at the end of the row with Heidi, Freya and Erica in between them.

"You look like sparrows on a wire," Luke muttered as he came closer and dumped the ledgers on the workbench across from them. Luke stood behind it like he was a college lecturer about to start his lesson.

"Is it exciting news?" Daisy asked, leaning forward to see what the ledgers were.

"Only you'd be excited about ledgers," Archer said at the end.

"You better hope I get excited about ledgers. Otherwise, you've hired the wrong accountant."

"True," Archer said, and the row nodded at the sentiment.

"What news do you have for us? I'm delighted Stan is nowhere to be seen," Jason said.

It was at that moment the door flew open and banged against the outside wall.

They all waited to see who was coming through, but no one did.

"No surfing today, Daisy, with that wind," Jason said to her left.

"Shame. I should have gone yesterday when it was calmer."

"People," Luke said, striding over to the door and pulling it closed, then clicking the safety feature on the push bar so it still worked, but the door was firmly closed.

"Well, get on with it," Daisy said.

"Mr Philbott died," Luke said.

"Oh no," Freya replied. "I really liked him."

"Who is Mr Philbott?" Archer asked.

"He was our pottery teacher," Freya said.

"He also was the island's stonemason," Jason added slowly. "What's in the ledgers?"

Luke grinned. "Every gravestone he made. Every gravestone his father made and back as far as the records were kept. He was old school and refused to use a computer."

"Okay, so why the dramatic family meeting?" Heidi asked.

"Ohh, shit, all the gravestones he made?" Daisy said.

"Yeah, including the two unmarked gravestones. The thing is, against every gravestone they built and put in place, either at Turner Hall or at the church's graveyard, it says who is buried in the plot."

"Shit," Archer said.

"Yes. The pieces of the puzzle are coming together," Luke replied.

"Can we have a recap and assume I wasn't here for six months of this puzzle expedition?" Daisy asked.

"Okay," Luke said, coming around to Daisy's side of the table and hopping onto his bench next to the ledgers. "Mrs Philbott said that she had secretly digitised all his records and wondered if we wanted to put these ledgers into the museum so people could look up their ancestors and see where they are buried. There is a separate one for the Turners, and she thought it would be best if we hung onto that one."

"Why?" Daisy asked, her curiosity piqued.

"Apparently, there's some sensitive information in there about the Turner family that Mrs Philbott didn't want to make public. She didn't give me any more details, but whatever it is, it must be pretty serious."

Daisy nodded, understanding the need for privacy. She had spent most of her life trying to keep her own family secrets hidden from the world.

"Have you looked?" Daisy asked.

Luke shook his head. "That's why I called this meeting. The handover was an hour ago. I think we should find out together who is in the unmarked graves."

Daisy wanted to text Nate and get him to the kitchens, but her brothers didn't know about him, and Luke would be less than impressed she was seeing her school bully. When Daisy thought too hard about it, she scared herself that she needed to have a bully around her at all times. Her history of growing up in Turner Hall with a bully. How the bullies treated her at school, and then college when she graduated ahead of time and then on the rigs where most of the men thought she was a liability just because she had a vagina.

It wasn't lost on her she was insanely attracted to the person who gave her hell when she was a teenager.

She shook her head, trying to clear her thoughts. Daisy was drawn to Nate's rough edges and his confidence despite her attempts to clear her thoughts of him. Remembering the men she had encountered on the rigs, the ones who thought she was weak because she was a woman. But Daisy was far from weak, and she knew it.

With a deep breath, she opened her mouth to speak, but Archer beat her to it.

"Open it," he said.

Luke picked up what she assumed was the Turner ledger and thumbed through the pages. It was half the size of the other ledgers and thin. For a family that had a lot of deaths, there didn't seem to be many pages. When Luke found what he was looking for, he scanned the page with his forefinger and then stabbed the page.

"Well, fucking hell," he said, giving a humourless laugh.

"Luke," Daisy snapped.

The others giggled at her impatience.

"All right, calm yourself. I thought Jason was the uptight one," Luke said.

Jason gave him the finger and then looped his arm around Freya's shoulder, bringing her in close. Jason's kiss on her temple reminded Daisy of Nate kissing her temple when she was scared out of her mind.

"We found the tin in the warehouse, and inside were the birth certificates of four children plus some other stuff that makes little sense right now."

"Like what?" Daisy asked.

"A list of plants and pesticides. I don't know why she would keep those with her children's birth certificates," Luke said.

Daisy went cold all over and gripped the edge of the workbench, stilling her legs.

"You okay?" Jason asked, resting his hand over hers.

"Yep," she said, repeatedly nodding.

With her other hand, she lifted her phone, held it to her face and then typed out a quick message. She tapped the side button and placed it back on the bench on her right side, where no one was sitting. No matter what they did as siblings, they sat in age order. No one was ever to her right side.

"What's the link?" Daisy stammered out, desperately trying to hold on to reality before she spaced out.

She could feel it coming.

"Cynthia buried her partner and son under those unmarked gravestones. They died six months before Archer came back to Copper Island. It looks like she buried them here."

"How did they die?" Erica asked.

Her voice sounded echoey, and all Daisy could focus on was the list of flowers and pesticides. Then she heard a faint hammering like a fist on a door. That's when she heard a commotion but was too far gone to work out what was happening.

It wasn't until warm lips touched hers that she came back to the present. She immediately threw her arms around Nate's neck and held on as he picked her up. She wrapped her legs around his waist, and he cradled her arse.

"Which way to her office?" she heard Nate say.

"What the fuck is going on here? You're the arsehole who made her life a misery at school."

That was Luke, she heard shouting at Nate.

"She has forgiven me. Now I'm making amends which is more than I can say for you lot. She's freaking out, and the furthest any of you are from her is ten feet. Jason, you're fucking well sitting next to her," he bellowed.

"How did you know she was freaking out?" Jason countered.

"She sent me an SOS."

"How did she know you would come?" he bantered back.

"Because I will always come for her," Nate roared. "You lot are so busy being loved up that you haven't noticed your goddamn sister could do with support. Now which fucking way to her office?"

"I'll take you," Erica said.

Daisy opened her eyes and saw Erica hop off the bench and lead the way. As Daisy passed Luke, Archer, Jason, Heidi and Freya, they all stroked her arm or back. But Daisy didn't have any energy to respond. She reserved all she had to hang on to Nate.

Nate followed Erica down the hall to Daisy's office, his heart racing with worry.

"What happened to cause her to send an SOS? Did any

of you hurt her? I'm going out of my mind here. Each possibility is more frightening than the last. I can't bear the thought of anything happening to her."

Daisy didn't know who he was talking to, but no one answered.

He had made her feel safe again.

When they finally arrived at her office, he barged in.

"Daisy?" he whispered, his voice barely above a whisper.

At the sound of his voice, Daisy's eyes shot open, and she looked at him with a mixture of relief and fear.

"Nate," she said, her voice shaking. "Thank God you came."

"Is she okay?" Archer asked.

Daisy was now in her office chair. She looked over Nate's shoulder as he crouched in front of her chair and saw her brothers and the girls standing on the threshold with faces of concern.

"I'll take care of her. She'll be fine with me," Nate said with authority.

"Come and knock on any of our cottages if you need us," Erica said.

Nate nodded and then focused his attention back on Daisy. His eyes were scanning her face but mainly concentrated on her eyes. She heard her office door click closed.

They were alone.

"You gave my brothers hell," Daisy said.

"I'm really unimpressed with the Turner boys. They were all up in my face in school because I was an arsehole to you, but now they're not looking out for you as adults. Fucking hell, Daisy, they were sitting within feet and didn't notice you silently panicking."

Daisy stared at him, mesmerised by his conviction, stunned by his vehemence.

"Thank you for coming."

"I will always come for you, always. I will always take care of you. I promise," he vowed.

She believed him. She wanted him to as well.

It was at that moment she knew she could love Nate. All she ever wanted was to be taken care of. Not just three weeks on an oil rig or from afar with her mother. She wanted full-time care, love, and passion and believed this man could give it to her.

Daisy couldn't help but feel a tingle run down her spine as he spoke those words with such sincerity. She knew he meant every single one of them, and it made her heart swell with happiness. For the first time in her life, she felt as if someone truly cared about her.

But as much as she wanted to give into the feeling and let him take care of her, there was still a nagging doubt at the back of her mind. What if he turned out to be just like all the others? What if he tired of her and left like everyone else had?

As if sensing her doubts, he reached out and took her hand, his touch sending shivers through her body.

"I know you're scared, Daisy," he said softly. "But I promise you, I will never leave you. I will always be here for you, no matter what."

She looked at him, her eyes searching his for any sign of deceit. But all she could see was genuine affection.

Daisy couldn't believe what she was feeling. She had never felt so safe and protected before. The way he looked at her, with such intensity and determination, made her heart race. She knew she wanted this man in her life forever.

As they sat together in her office, Daisy felt her body respond to his touch. His hands were strong yet gentle as he ran his fingers through her hair. She leaned in closer, wanting to feel his lips on hers.

Without a word, he kissed her deeply, his tongue exploring her mouth. Daisy moaned softly, lost in the passion that he was igniting within her. She could feel his desire for her as his hands roamed over her body.

As they pulled away from each other, they were both breathless. Daisy looked into his eyes and knew this was the man she wanted to spend the rest of her life with. He was the one who would take care of her, protect her, and love her always.

She was sure of it.

"Is it inappropriate that I want to lock that door, close the blinds and have my way with you?" he said, his eyes glittering.

If she was in a better state, she would've hopped up onto her desk and pulled him between her legs. But she needed to get a grip on why she kept freaking out.

"I promise we'll have desk sex at some stage," she promised.

She was promising more than sex, and his face shone like she'd given him the best present in the world.

Nate wanted her as much as she wanted him.

12

Nate

Nate stepped into the pub. He chose the quieter of the two pubs on Copper Island because he wanted a quiet evening. The Crown pub had a rowdy lot most nights. Looking around the dimly lit room, he saw the usual faces who also wanted a quiet pint.

It was a Thursday night, a few days after he'd carried Daisy out of Edward Hall kitchens. The bar was fairly empty, with just a few patrons scattered around the tables. He was looking for a drink and his best friend's counsel.

A beer would do the trick.

He scanned the bar, but his gaze was quickly drawn to one particular booth in the corner, where his best mate Selly was already sitting. A smile flashed across his face as he greeted him warmly, and he eagerly took the spot across from him, eager to catch up.

Selly looked up and smiled at Nate. "Hey, how's the wrist?"

"It was just a sprain. All healed, thankfully."

"Thank fuck for that. I felt bad even though it was an accident."

"At least it gets me out of rowing practice for a while. You want another?" Nate asked, looking at his friend's glass that only had an inch of beer in it.

"Yeah, a pint of bitter, mate," Selly said, holding up his glass. "They can reuse this one."

"I think it's a myth that it tastes better if the same glass is used," Nate grumbled.

Selly laughed as he walked away. Nate had been friends with Selly and Rob since they were children, and they both shared a deep love of rowing and beer. Nate was the serious one, Rob the outlandish one, and Selly was somewhere in the middle to balance them out.

When Nate returned with two pints and a packet of crisps between his teeth, Selly squinted at him. His friend waited for him to sit on the opposite seat and then spoke.

"What's been happening, Nate? I haven't seen you in a while," he asked, his voice full of concern.

Nate sighed. He hadn't intended for it to come out, but the words tumbled from his lips before he could stop them.

"I've fallen in love with someone, Selly," he said, his voice thick with emotion.

Selly's brow furrowed. "Who? I saw you a few weeks ago, and you were single then."

Nate paused, his gaze flicking away from him. "Daisy Turner," he said, his voice barely above a whisper.

Selly's eyes widened in surprise. Daisy Turner was not someone Nate would have expected to be interested in, let alone fall in love with. Selly knew that too.

Daisy was from a completely different background, and

they had never even spoken to each other since he'd taunted her at school fifteen years ago.

"Wow," Selly said. He paused for a moment, studying his face. "Do you... Do you think she feels the same?"

Nate shrugged. "I don't know. We've not talked about it. But I can't stop thinking about her..." His voice trailed off, and he stared down at the table, lost in his thoughts.

Selly reached across the table, opened the crisps and sat back with a grin.

"You never know," he said. "Maybe it's fate?"

Nate smiled slightly, but someone still tinged his expression with sadness.

"Maybe," he said. "If someone had said while I was in school that I'd be hot for her when I was an adult, I would laugh in their faces. Rob was his usual self in front of her a few weeks ago, and she retreated like she'd gone back in time. She recognised him, but he had no clue who she was."

"I'd heard about that. Rob feels awful. Has she changed that much?"

"Yeah, big time. She was always pretty, but now she's beautiful, confident and get this? She drives a forklift truck like she was born to do it."

Selly gave him a rueful smile. "I wondered how you were able to still keep up the deliveries with your wrist injury."

"Yeah, she helped me out big time."

"So, are you going to ask her out on a date?"

"That's the weird thing. We've spent time with each other like we're friends, but I know we both feel it's deeper than that. Asking her now out on a date will seem odd. Plus, I don't want to scare her off. I'd rather keep her as a friend."

"Have you run into her aunt yet at the Hall?"

"No, Daisy and her brothers live in the cottages on the

estate, and she doesn't go anywhere near her. I'm not sure what the story is, but she hates her aunt."

"She belongs to a very large club," Selly said and took a gulp of his pint. "Oh fuck, looks like we have company. Do you want me to stay?" Selly said, eyeing the door that had opened.

NATE LOOKED over his shoulder to see who had walked in. Archer, Jason and Luke strode in, looking pensive. They scanned the bar, and their eyes landed on Nate. His heart began to race, and he felt a wave of anger sweep over him. What were they doing there?

"Up to you, mate. This shouldn't take long," Nate replied, turning fully to face them.

"I'll stay. Two against three will never work, especially with your wrist, but I'll give it my best."

Nate turned his head and gave his friend a smirk. "Thanks, mate."

The brothers approached their table, and Archer spoke first.

"We're here to have a word with you," he said, his voice low and menacing.

Nate stood up, his hands fisting. He had no idea what they would say, but he knew it wouldn't be friendly.

Nate's eyes narrowed. "What exactly is it you want?" he asked, his voice full of defiance.

Archer glanced at Selly and then turned back to Nate.

"We want to know what you're doing with our sister," he said. "We just want to make sure you understand that this is not acceptable. She deserves better than someone like you."

Nate fury raised its head. He stepped into Archer's space. Nate noticed Jason and Luke flank him, and the pub grew quiet. Whatever went down would be island gossip within minutes. When Jason punched his old long-time friend, Keith, it spread like wildfire within minutes.

"This is what's going to happen. I'm going to ask you three questions about Daisy. If you get two out of three right, we can have your chat. If you can't answer at least two of them, then we're done talking, and you can leave me the fuck alone. Are you up for it?" Nate asked, looking at each of them in turn.

"What are the questions?" Jason said. "This should be a breeze. We're her brothers."

Nate ignored the arrogance.

"Question one. Daisy volunteers three nights a week and a shift at the weekend. What does she do?"

Nate was met with a trio of blank faces. Archer looked to Jason and then Luke, but they didn't answer.

"You can confer. I don't mind," Nate said, his words dripping with derision.

Selly laughed into his pint behind Nate, and that drew a smirk to Nate's face.

"No? Don't know? All right. Let's try an easier one. When did Daisy finish her work experience?"

Another set of furrowed brows and shaking of heads.

"Jesus fuck, what the hell have you been doing?" Nate asked.

"Now listen," Luke said, pointing a finger.

Nate ignored the tone and ploughed on. "Last question. How many blackouts has Daisy had like the one you witnessed?"

"Two," Archer said confidently.

"Any advances on two?" Nate asked Luke and Jason.

Both men shook their heads.

"You're wrong. You three should be ashamed of yourselves. Arseholes the lot of you. Now you get to leave me alone. I warn you, do not approach Daisy and warn her off me. You no longer have that right."

Nate turned his back on the brothers, gulped down half his pint, and then stared at his friend. Selly looked over his shoulder and tracked the brothers' movements until Nate heard the pub door slam shut. The brothers hadn't slammed the door. It was how the hinge worked at that pub. Still, it made him jump.

"I can't believe they couldn't answer any of the questions. I always thought those siblings were tight."

"I'm getting the impression nothing is what we thought it was with the Turners," Nate said. "Another?" he asked.

"Yeah, but I'll get this round."

13

Daisy

Daisy quickly became accustomed to the two types of team meetings Archer called. They met in his office on the first floor if it had to do with Edward Hall. If it was strictly Turner business, then they met in the kitchen where comfort food was on tap.

The meeting that day would be in Archer's office. Daisy didn't know what to expect. It had been a week since she'd had her panic attack, and she hadn't spoken to any of them. She hadn't spoken to Nate either, choosing to work long hours with her day job at Edward Hall and taking extra shifts for the helpline in the evenings.

Daisy hesitated outside Archer's office, taking deep breaths to calm her racing heart. She had avoided everyone for a week, but now it was time to face them. She knocked softly on the door and heard Archer's voice calling her in.

As Daisy stepped into Archer's office, she felt a knot form in her stomach. He sat at his desk, staring at his computer screen. He looked up as Daisy walked in and motioned for her to take a seat. As she entered the room, she saw only Archer was present. Daisy greeted him with a nod, feeling the knot in her stomach tighten. Archer motioned again for her to take a seat, and she sat down, feeling like a prisoner waiting for her sentence.

"I hope you're feeling better now," Archer said as she sat down.

Daisy nodded, unsure of what to say.

"I called you here because I wanted to talk to you about Nate," Archer continued.

"I thought this was our monthly meeting?"

"It is, but that starts in fifteen minutes. I sent a message to Jason and Luke to come by a little later so I could talk to you."

"Oh. Well, we're partners in this business, and you're making this into a boss and subordinate meeting. So if this is about me, why are we having this meeting in your office?"

"Because you've been avoiding me."

This was true. She timed it so that she wasn't around when Archer picked up Teddy. Daisy had also taken to locking her back door.

"Are you feeling better, Daisy?" Archer asked, his voice gentle.

Daisy nodded, unable to meet his gaze. She had been avoiding him for a reason. She didn't want to face the consequences of her weakness the day the gravestones were revealed. It had nothing to do with the gravestones and everything to do with the tin and its contents. She wasn't ready to tell him she was in contact with their mother.

"I'm sorry for avoiding you," she finally said, her voice barely above a whisper. "I just needed some time to myself."

Archer reached across the table. "You don't have to apologise to me. You're my little sister, and it took Nate's speech to see I've been neglecting you. You have always been so far ahead of us in maturity every year growing up. It never occurred to me you might be suffering."

"It's fine. I'm just dealing with some stuff that I can't figure out."

"Will you tell me about it?"

"Not now. I want to get it straight in my head, and then I can talk to you all."

With a gentle smile, Archer reached out and took his sister's hand in his.

"Just know that we're all here for you, no matter what. You can always come to me, okay? I'll be your rock."

Daisy's eyes filled with tears, and she squeezed his hand back. She had found another rock while her brothers were making a life with the women they'd fallen in love with. Still, it was good for Daisy to know they'd be there for her when she revealed her secret.

"Thank you, Archer. You have no idea how much that means to me."

"Okay, whenever you're ready."

Daisy sat in silence for a moment, staring at her brother. She knew she had to tell him eventually, but the thought of revealing her secret made her stomach churn. How would she tell him she had been in touch with their mother her whole life?

Archer sensed his sister's hesitation and gently squeezed her hand. "Whatever it is, you can tell me," he said softly.

A knock on the door interrupted them, and then it opened. Jason stuck his head around the door.

"Safe to come in?" Jason asked.

"Of course, it's safe to go in," Luke said, shoving him

aside. "She's our sister. We gave him fifteen minutes to be big responsible brother. Now we get to be the nice guys."

As soon as Jason entered the room, the tension between Daisy and her brother, Archer, disappeared. She cleared her throat, trying to break the awkward atmosphere.

"Hey, what's going on?" she asked, looking from Luke to Jason.

"I'm fine. He's fine," Jason said, thumbing to Luke. "What's going on with you and Nathaniel Hill?"

Daisy spoke, her voice shaking slightly. "We've been spending time together," she said. "I know none of you will approve."

Archer scoffed. "Well, you're right about that," he said. "Nathaniel is bad news, Daisy. You can't trust him."

Jason nodded in agreement. "He's got a reputation for using women and then tossing them aside," he said. "You don't want to get involved with someone like that."

Daisy bristled at their words. "I can make my own decisions," she said defiantly. "And Nate isn't like that. He's kind and caring, and he treats me well."

Luke, who had been quiet until now, spoke up. "I agree with Jason," he said. "Nathaniel is not a good guy."

"You guys are just judging him based on rumours," Daisy said. "You should hear the rumours about us and none of them are true.

Luke, Jason and Archer exchanged a look, clearly not convinced.

Daisy shifted in her seat while the others took theirs around the small conference table. She felt her face flame with anger. Daisy couldn't believe that her brothers were being so judgmental about Nathaniel. She had never felt this way about anyone before, and she knew deep down that he differed from the other guys she had dated in the past.

"I can't believe you guys," she said, her voice trembling with emotion. "You don't even know him, and yet you're ready to label him as a bad guy just because of some stupid comments when we were in school."

"Those comments made you cry, Daisy," Luke said.

"He's different now. Anyway, this meeting is about Edward Hall, not my love life. I didn't interfere with yours, so keep out of mine."

Daisy stood up, her hands resting on the table as she leaned forward to stare at her brothers.

"You don't get to judge me, Luke. You don't get to decide who I love or who I date. Nathaniel has been nothing but kind and understanding towards me, something that none of my brothers have been able to do."

Her brothers recoiled in surprise at her sudden outburst. She had always been the quiet one in the family, the peacemaker who avoided confrontations. But not this time. She was tired of being dismissed and belittled by her own family.

"Let's get this meeting started so I can go back to my desk to make sure we can pay our wages bill this month," she barked.

She watched her brothers attempt to disagree and want to grill her about Nate, but she was all business, banging open her work diary with the list of subjects she wanted to go through. Archer would give his headline news, and then it would be Daisy.

Luke gave her the evils, and Jason had moved on and tapped at his tablet to get to come to life. When she looked back to Archer, he was giving her a look of contemplation. A look she couldn't read.

As the meeting progressed, Daisy could feel Archer's gaze on her. It was as if he was studying her, trying to decipher what had caused her sudden change in demeanour. Daisy couldn't help but feel self-conscious under his scrutiny.

When it was finally her turn to speak, she took a deep breath and began to go through her list of subjects. But she couldn't shake off the feeling that Archer was still watching her intently.

When she was done, Archer went to his updates.

"Some Turner business that links in with Edward Hall that you should know," Archer said. "Jennifer has retired, and Cynthia has hired nurses to look after her."

Daisy's dating life and her panic attacks were forgotten. They all focussed on Archer. Jennifer had been by Cynthia's side for fifty years or more.

"Was it over the row outside the cottages?" Daisy asked and then regretted her omission.

"How do you know about that?" Luke asked.

"I was there," Daisy confessed.

"We didn't see you. In fact, we didn't see you for a month afterwards."

"I didn't hang around. My internship finished early, so I came back to Copper Island. I could see something going down and decided if I was coming back full time, then I should take a break before coming back."

"For a month?" Jason said.

"It was a really nice hotel," Daisy replied with a shrug.

Three sets of wary glances swung her way, but Archer spoke up again.

"I'm told by Bailey that she only goes out for fresh air at night. Don't be alarmed if you see her wandering about for fresh air at night. She's taken to walking the perimeter of the fencing along the cliff after the filming shuts down for the day."

Daisy's body went stiff. She now knew what had set her off. She had seen her aunt. Daisy hadn't spoken to her aunt since Archer's wedding and the signing over of Edward Hall. It was enough to set her off.

"Daisy, are you okay?" Archer asked. "Are you having another attack?"

Daisy took a deep breath and cleared her throat, trying to push away the discomfort of her brothers' gazes. She knew they were waiting for her to say something. She couldn't.

Daisy wanted to pick up her phone and send a message to Nate, but a business meeting wasn't the time.

"I'm fine. First on my list," she began, flipping through her diary, "is the finances for the marketing campaign for the regatta next Spring. We need to start planning the launch event and coordinate with the advertising team to create a buzz."

Luke groaned, rolling his eyes. "Can't we just hire someone else to handle that? I don't have time for that."

Daisy shot him a glare. "We can't afford to outsource everything, Luke. Plus, this is a crucial part of the business. We need to make sure the launch is successful in generating revenue for Copper Island."

Archer nodded in agreement, a hint of a smile on his lips.

Daisy felt a small sense of relief that at least one of her brothers was letting her off.

14

Daisy

It was a beautiful late autumn day. The sea was calm, and Daisy was itching to get out onto the water. She was shocked that Nate had never been surfing, so she set about righting that wrong. She was waiting on her back patio for him to arrive when Erica came strolling along with Isobel.

Daisy tossed her book on the sofa and launched towards them.

"Aren't you looking cute in your onesie," Daisy said to Isobel, and Erica handed her over.

She kissed the apple of Isobel's cheek and then smothered the little girl until she giggled.

"You going surfing?" Erica asked, sitting on the wall, stretching her legs out towards the lawn.

Daisy joined her, bouncing Isobel on her thigh.

"Yeah. Nate's joining me. He's never been before."

Erica raised an eyebrow. "Really? Nate's never been

surfing before? That's surprising, considering he practically grew up on the beach and rows," she said, her eyes scanning the horizon. "Well, I hope he's a quick learner. The waves can be pretty unforgiving this time of year."

Daisy shrugged. "He'll be fine. Besides, I'll be there to teach him," she said with a smirk. "I'm a pretty excellent teacher."

Erica laughed. "I'm sure you are. Just make sure you don't distract him too much."

Daisy rolled her eyes. "I'll try not to," she said, standing up and handing Isobel back to Erica. "I should go get my board ready. Nate should be here any minute."

As Daisy walked towards the rack on the wall to get her board, she felt a thrill of excitement. She loved surfing, loved the feeling of the wind in her hair and the rush of adrenaline as she caught a wave.

Just as she was about to grab her board, she heard her name being called out.

She peeked over the patio wall, hanging onto the wooden support post for the trestle and saw Nate walking along the path a little nervously. Daisy grinned to herself. She loved the idea of being the one to introduce him to something new.

"That's my cue to head off for a saunter around the lawns," Erica said, leaning in to kiss Daisy's cheek.

"See you soon," Daisy replied, kissing them both.

"You've been a stranger, come by for dinner this week," Erica said, giving her a mum look.

"I will."

Nate had reached them. He gave Isobel a tickle under her chin. She rewarded him with a gurgle and a mass of bubbles.

"See you later. Wear sunscreen," Erica called out over her shoulder.

When Erica was out of view, Nate leaned in and gave Daisy a long slow kiss that set her nerves on end.

When they broke apart, she picked up her board.

"I'm glad you made it."

"I should tell you that I'm clumsy when I'm on the water."

"You'll be fine with me. I'll take care of you."

Nathan grabbed her hand and smiled.

They walked down the uneven planks half covered in sand, hand in hand.

Nate smiled, but she could see the nervousness in his eyes. "I'm a little nervous, to be honest."

Daisy gave him a reassuring grin. "Don't worry, I'll be right there with you. And the waves aren't too big today, so it'll be perfect for beginners."

Nate nodded, taking a deep breath. "Okay, let's do this."

Daisy led the way towards the beach, carrying her board with ease. Nate followed close behind, still looking a little apprehensive. As they reached the shore, Daisy turned back to Nate.

"Okay, first things first. Let me show you how to paddle out."

She showed him the proper technique, lying chest down on her board and using her arms to push herself through the water. Nate watched carefully and then tried it for himself.

"Good, good," Daisy said encouragingly. "Now, when you see a wave coming, you're going to turn around and start paddling towards shore. And when you feel the wave lift you up, you're going to pop up to your feet and ride it all the way in."

Nate nodded, taking it all in. Daisy could see the determination in his eyes.

"Okay, ready to give it a try?" she asked, and Nate nodded again.

Daisy could feel the tension radiating off of Nate, but she didn't let it show that she could sense it. Instead, she chatted cheerfully about the waves and the technique she would teach him.

She showed him how to lie on the board and paddle out when they got to the water. The waves were small, but they still had a bit of power to them. Daisy watched as Nate struggled to navigate the whitewater, his movements awkward and jerky.

"Relax," she called out to him. "You're not going to fall off. Just paddle out further."

Nate nodded, taking a deep breath and working on his technique. After a few minutes, they made it out past the break, and Daisy showed him how to position himself on the board.

"Okay, now just wait for the right wave and paddle hard. I'll be right behind you," she said.

Nate took a deep breath and nodded, looking out at the sea. Daisy watched as he scanned the horizon, trying to anticipate the next wave. She could see the determination in his eyes, and it made her heart sing.

Suddenly, she saw a swell rising in the distance. "There, Nate, go for that one!" she called out, pointing towards the wave.

Nate paddled hard. Daisy was right behind him, feeling the wave, urging him to pop up to his feet. He struggled at first, wobbling on the board, but then he found his balance and rode the wave all the way to shore.

Daisy cheered him on, feeling a rush of excitement. She

watched as Nate jumped off the board, grinning from ear to ear.

"That was amazing!" he exclaimed, running his hands through his hair. "I can't believe I actually did it."

Daisy laughed. "I told you, surfing is the best. And you're a natural. Are you ready to do it again?"

Nate sat up, nodding eagerly. "Absolutely. Let's go."

And with that, they dove back into the water.

After an hour, Daisy was wiped. It had been too long since she'd surfed, and she didn't have working on the rigs for weeks on end to keep her strength up. Daisy signalled for them to head to the shore. Once they were on dry land, they dragged their boards up to the flat near the rocks and retrieved the picnic bag she'd brought.

Daisy and Nate were sitting on a blanket spread out on the flat rocks of the beach. The day was unseasonably warm, and the sun shone down on them, making the sand glisten. All around them were stretches of beach and not much else, giving them a sense of privacy.

Nate reached out to take Daisy's hand and gently squeezed it. He smiled at her and asked, "So, Daisy, tell me what you used to do on your off weeks from the rigs? What did you do you do for fun?"

Daisy's brown hair fell in a mess around her face while her eyes stared blankly at the afternoon sky. She fell back onto the blanket with a handful of grapes in her hand, popping one into her mouth while she thought about the question. The grapes were sweet and cold from the refrigerator.

The sun was warm but not warm enough to unzip the top of her wetsuit like Nate had. She turned her head to admire his muscled for a second and caught the sexy smirk he was sending her way.

"Well, as soon as the helicopter dropped the four of us off, we went to the house we lived in up in Scotland. We had one day to decompress, which was usually sleeping and washing clothes. Then we would pack, have dinner with our next-door neighbour, then set off on our trip overseas."

"You were close to your neighbour?"

"You could say that," Daisy said and closed her eyes.

Nate moved closer to thread his fingers with hers.

"Tell me?"

"Our neighbour is actually our mother, but my brothers don't know."

"Fuck," Nate bit out. "When they find out, they are not going to react well."

"No, they'll probably be very disappointed in me."

"It's not on you, Daisy. There is nothing wrong with wanting to be near your mum. Mine is on the mainland, and I only get to see her once a month. I can't really leave Copper Island for any length of time because it means closing the workshop, and I need every bit of business I can get my hands on. They come across to me. So I know the need to be near your parents, and you only have one."

"My family is so complex and dark. You really should think twice about starting anything with me, Nate."

"I'm not going anywhere. I can handle anything you throw at me. My mind has wild ideas about why a mother would leave her four children and husband. It has to be extreme."

"She didn't leave my dad. They were still together."

"How did they manage that?"

"We had a routine. My dad worked on the rigs with us for three weeks, and then we would have three weeks off. None of us wanted to go to Copper Island in our downtime, so we went away overseas for three weeks. Sometimes near and sometimes far, depending on the time of year and the cost of travel. Our dad said he would hole up at the house for a few days to relax and then head down to Copper Island to do Turner work."

"He must have been exhausted."

"We all saw him age faster than his years. We begged him to sign over the inheritance to his sister, Cynthia, but he wouldn't hear of it. Saying that it was what she wanted and he would never give her what she wanted."

"So, how were they still together?"

"He stayed for the first three days of every time off to be with Mum. We had flown off somewhere, so they had seclusion for three days."

"I'm heartbroken for your mum. That must have been hard on the both of them."

"My mum said she was happy to see him at all after what she went through. She didn't tell me the finer details, but she did let slip once what Cynthia did to her to make her move off the island."

Daisy stayed quiet and was glad Nate didn't ask her what that was because she couldn't cope with saying it out loud.

"I admire you, Daisy. You're made of strong stuff."

"I think that's probably the problem with these flashbacks. I wish they'd just come to the surface so I don't have to be scared all the time."

"It will come out when it's ready. I'll be there when it does. The upside of living on a small island," Nate said and smiled.

Nate leaned closer and kissed her lightly on the lips. Daisy felt her heart flutter as they both smiled, and she leaned in to kiss him back. The sun shone down on them as they kissed, and the water lapped at the shore.

Daisy felt herself igniting with passion as Nate's hands

explored her body, sending shivers down her spine. She moaned softly into his mouth as their tongues danced together in a fiery dance. The warmth of the sun, the coolness of the water, and the intensity of their kiss all merged into one glorious moment.

Nate's hands slid down her waist, pulling her closer to him. Daisy could feel the hardness of his body against hers, and she knew she wanted him more than anything else in the world right now. With a fierce desire burning within her, she broke the kiss and whispered into his ear, "We have to stop. This is too public."

Nate broke the kiss and whispered in Daisy's ear, "Let's take this somewhere more private."

Daisy nodded, and Nate took her hand, leading her towards a secluded spot on the beach. Once they were hidden, Nate pressed Daisy up against a tree and kissed her again. This time, his hands roamed freely, teasing and exploring her body.

He pulled the zip of her wetsuit down to reveal she wore no bikini top. Nate's hand slid inside, and she closed her eyes as he cupped her breast.

"Fucking hell, Daisy, you're perfect."

Daisy wanted Nate with so much intensity she arched her back and pressed herself closer to him. She could feel his hardness against her and knew she wanted him.

Nate lifted Daisy up without a word, holding her against the tree and pressing against her as he kissed her. Her heart was pumping so fast she couldn't get close enough. Her legs tightened around his waist, searching for friction.

They were wearing too many clothes.

"We could go back to the cottage?" she said.

"Are you sure, Daisy?"

"Never surer of anything, Nate."

Nate nodded, not saying a word, and slowly lowered Daisy to the ground. They collected the surfboards and packed up their picnic. He took her hand, and they began walking back towards the cottage. As they walked, Nate's thumb gently grazed the back of Daisy's hand, sending sparks of electricity through her body.

15

Nate

They left the surfboards on the floor in the back patio area and dumped the picnic bags on the kitchen island.

Once their hands were free, Nate pulled Daisy close for a deep kiss. This was it. This was going to rock his world. He just knew it.

"Daisy," he whispered, trailing his lips over her throat.

He had to know before he sank into her.

"Nate," she whispered back, banding an arm around his back as he coaxed her to take the stairs.

"We've never talked about what we are," he said.

She was a stair above him as they climbed, making them the same height. He pulled down the zipper of her wetsuit, revealing her glorious tits for him to tease and squeeze.

"I don't want to be with anyone else, Nate. I feel like I've been waiting for you."

His hands roamed her body as if it was his own personal playground. His touch was gentle, yet determined to get her naked. He'd already seen every inch of her from their bath together, but this was different.

Nate's lips travelled down her neck, leaving a trail of goose pimples in its wake. Once they were completely naked, Nate lifted Daisy into his arms and carried her to the bedroom, where he gently laid her down on the bed.

Nate cupped her face with his large warm hands. He hoped they weren't too rough to the touch. She hadn't mentioned his calloused hands, but then Daisy had worked on the rigs for years.

"This is going to be hard for me not to show you the raw version of Nathaniel Hill," he said. "You're so beautiful. I can't control how much I want you."

His dick was painfully hard, but he was determined to make this last as long as possible.

"I want all versions of you. Pick one, and I'll be there with you. We'll have plenty of time for gentle. I need you like I never knew I needed you."

"Jesus, Daisy," he exclaimed.

Nate leaned in and pressed his lips gently to hers. He kept them there, melting against her mouth. Nate kept kissing Daisy's lips, taking it slowly, waiting for her to take the next step. He had wanted to fuck her the first night they met but knew from experience not to push someone who wasn't ready. Now that he had the green light, fucking her was no longer what he wanted. Nate wanted to claim her, so she'd never leave him.

He dropped his hands, circled her back with his arms, and pulled her close, kissing her more forcefully. Daisy responded and moved her tongue along his lower lip. It was a tentative, nervous exploration to take charge, even for a second or two. Like every time they kissed, on the second sweep, Nate had opened his mouth and met her tongue with his. Both of them let out a long exhale through their noses and breathed in deeply as they opened their mouths to get closer still. The heat in the room increased. She wrapped her arms around his neck and pulled at his hair as she threaded her fingers through his locks.

Nate broke the kiss first and kissed her neck, pressing firm closed kisses until he reached the curve of her shoulder. He threaded their fingers as he kissed his way down to her chest.

"I want you so much, Daisy, what about condoms?"

"I'm on birth control," she said and sighed as he took a nipple into his mouth.

It hardened instantly.

He kissed up her neck and to her earlobe, biting gently and whispering again in her ear.

"You want nothing between us?" he asked, nibbling and blowing gently into her ear.

"Nothing," she said.

It was a hoarse reply, her voice shaking as she shivered in response to his touch.

"Slide into me. I want to feel all of you," Daisy said, lifting her hips to brush her pussy against his stomach.

"All in good time," Nate answered.

Daisy roughly grabbed his neck, pulled him to her, and forcedly kissed him. She held the back of his head while she took what he was giving.

Nate reciprocated and held her close while she kissed him. Then gently, he turned them so she as she sat astride him and didn't stop kissing her mouth. Her passion took hold of her body, and she guided her legs to fit either side of his hips snugly.

Nate grabbed her bottom and brought her close to his pelvis, his hard erection straining to be inside her. Daisy swivelled her hips on his lap, looking for friction with a sexy smile.

She was fabulously naked, looming above him, her breasts moving as she gyrated her hips. He'd never forget this view, wishing he could snap a picture of her lust-filled face.

Nate dropped one of his hands to slide between them, and using his thumb, he rubbed her clit through her slick folds. He was rewarded with a moan. Her mouth opened wide while she watched Nate's hand stop rubbing and slide out of sight and inside her. Inserting his thumb, he found her wet entrance and gently pushed it in and out methodically. Her cries of pleasure rang out, and Nate closed his eyes, listening to Daisy moan and feel her pussy clamp tighter around his thumb. He pulled out his thumb and replaced it with two fingers, pumping her more frantically.

He wanted to watch her come undone.

Daisy grabbed his shoulders for balance and met his fingers, thrust for thrust. She bounced on his lap until her orgasm started to build, and the waves began to cascade over his fingers. Then she stopped her movements, leaving her on the edge of detonation. A hot flush spread over her body, and she stilled.

"Stop moving, Nate. I want you inside me when I come," she said.

Nate wasted no time in caressing her once again. Kneading and squeezing her breasts, getting used to how sensitive Daisy was to his touch. The skin around her nipples pebbled, and goose pimples covered her in a wave.

His erection bobbed between them, and Daisy stroked him softly. The drop of fluid smearing over her fingers was nearly his undoing.

Daisy clambered off his lap and turned her back to him, flicking her long hair over her shoulders.

"Where are you going?" Nate squeaked out.

"Are you sure you want this?" she said and hurried to the windows to close the curtains.

There was no way anyone could see in, but he wasn't about to call her out on it. Then she put her hand on the armchair near the window and kept her back to him, waiting for his answer.

"Fuck, yeah, I do."

He palmed his hard cock with one hand, casually stroking it up and down.

His taut stomach bunched in his slouched position, and his knees were wide apart. He was over the moon that his beautiful woman wanted to move their relationship to a more intimate level. Nate continued to stroke his cock, waiting for her next move. His orgasm was beginning to build.

Daisy's round, pert bottom begged to be nibbled, and he moved from the bed while she had her back to him.

Crawling on his hands and knees, he had reached her within four feet. Leaning down to her ankles, he kissed his way up her left leg alternating from the inside of her leg to the outside. He licked her sensory spot when he reached the joint at the back of her knee. Kneeling up, he faced her derriere and kissed each cheek while reaching his hands around to hold on to her thighs and held on tight.

"Bend over, sweetheart and hold on to the back of the chair," he said to her, holding the flat of one of his hands on the base of her back, urging her to bend forward.

She did as he asked, and he could see her pussy lips glistening, wet and inviting. He licked and probed while continually stroking his cock. She mewled in approval, pushing back on his tongue and gained momentum as her orgasm started to build once more.

"Can we move to the bed? I don't think I can stand anymore," Daisy asked and stood back upright.

She thoroughly enjoyed what Nate's tongue was doing, if her arousal was anything to go by, but her knees were weakening.

"Of course," Nate said and tugged her by the hand to the bed.

She dutifully followed slowly. Turning, she positioned him so that she could give him a gentle push. He fell back and sat on the bed, grinning up at her. Nate palmed his cock once more, not breaking eye contact.

He could have got off just by looking at her, but he wanted to be inside her.

"Now you have me where you want me? What are you going to do next?" Nate asked.

Daisy didn't answer him. Instead, she turned, grabbed a cushion from the armchair, and held it against her body. She nodded to his knees, and he obediently parted them. Daisy dropped the pillow between his ankles and knelt down, placing her hands on his hairy thighs for balance.

"Put your hands above your head and do not move them. If they come anywhere near my head, I'll stop. I don't like my head being held," she murmured as she brushed her lips along his inner thigh.

"Yes, ma'am," he said and immediately let go of his cock and interlinked his fingers and put them on his head.

He would've agreed to anything.

Daisy leaned forward, keeping her hands on his thighs,

and she smoothed them up further to his hips and let her hair fall forward. The sensation of the soft feather-like touches stiffened Nate's dick once more. Her hair had covered her face and his cock, making it difficult to see when she would take him into her mouth. Daisy didn't move her hands and instead used her tongue to seek out the tip of his cock.

She licked from his base to his tip using the flat of her tongue. He groaned at the contact and dropped his head back onto the bed. There was no point looking. He widened his legs further and shifted on the mattress to enjoy Daisy's mouth around his hard, throbbing cock.

She had taken him inside her mouth, pointing her tongue and using it to tease the underside of his head. She licked away the droplets that were forming very slowly, letting them drip for a few seconds. The frustration started to build in Nate's groin. He wanted to release hot liquid into her mouth for her to swallow. What he wanted more was to feel how warm her pussy would be around his cock.

"I want to be inside you, Daisy. I can't hold back much longer. Please come and sit on my lap," he pleaded.

Pushing back her hair from her face and tucking the stray hairs behind her ear, Daisy licked her lips and grinned at Nate.

"Fuck," he whispered, staring at the goddess before him.

Daisy nodded, and he shifted back on the bed. She straddled his lap, keeping his cock between their stomachs. Then Daisy kissed him, slowly, languid kisses, taking her time to get to know his mouth, playing hide and seek with her tongue. She goaded him to come into her mouth, retracting her tongue and then starting the tango to entwine their mouths.

He didn't know who was leading this sexy dance, and he didn't much care. Daisy was in his arms, naked.

While she teased and taunted him, she held onto his erection, ensuring he got stiffer each minute that passed. Slow strokes up and down, her thumb swiping his tip, she kept going until his continued groans grew louder. His thrusts into her hand turned were getting frantic.

His eyes were narrowed on her, but he didn't say a word, silently pleading with her to get a move on. Nate watched with fascination as her hand rested on his shoulder for balance, and then she knelt up and positioned the tip of his cock at her entrance.

Once she was sure that he was safely in by an inch, she placed both of her hands on his shoulders. Nate grabbed both of her breasts roughly and held on tight. He had her nipples clamped between his finger and thumb.

She dropped down and impaled herself, Nate timed it perfectly, and when he had all his cock inside her, he squeezed hard on her nipples. She cried out her pleasure and gave as good as she got. She started to swivel her hips in a circle, getting used to his size and getting him to push deeper inside her. She parted her knees further so she could take him deeper still. Once she was happy, she started to move up and down, her short nails digging into his shoulders as she used them to support her body.

Harder and harder, she fell on his cock, needing the friction to build her orgasm. Nate could feel every inch of him expanding as he grew harder.

Nate kept one breast in his hand, kneading roughly while he took her other nipple into his mouth and sucked hard. He had to concentrate on her moves and coordinate his teasing. He lost his grip as she moved faster. The slapping sound of her bottom hitting his thighs helped him keep pace. After a while, he gave up and watched as Daisy bit her lip when she was nearly at her breaking point. He let go first, spilling all he had into her, yelling his release as he continued to watch her enjoy his hard cock.

He had started to soften, and she still hadn't come, but she continued to bounce. He found her clit and rubbed circles around it without touching it. In seconds she let out a strangled cry. The waves that rippled over his cock caused it to twitch inside her. He was halfway to his next orgasm.

Her euphoric smile prompted his balls to tighten and begin the glorious journey to another orgasm, he didn't know if he could come again so soon, but he would put his best effort into it.

Switching their positions deftly, he had her on her back and withdrew from her. She rested, spread on the bed before him. He kneeled back at the end of the mattress and stroked his cock once more. Daisy played with herself, gently circling her clit while she watched him create another hard erection. She grabbed her breast roughly like he had, but it wasn't the same if he couldn't pinch her nipples.

He could see the red marks where his hand had been.

"I need to do that again, Daisy. Are you ready?" he asked and leaned forward.

"Hurry, I miss your hands on my skin."

Positioning himself once more at her entrance, he lay over her body and kissed her, inching in further as he worshipped her lips with his mouth. Nate raised her thighs, encouraging her to wrap her legs around his waist. Once he had her where he wanted her, he rested his elbows on the bed next to her arms and rocked gently in and out of her body. His mouth nuzzled her neck as he brought them both to the height of their second orgasm. Daisy came quietly this time. The softer throbs of her climax took hold of his cock and squeezed until he came. Her walls contracted until she heard his muffled groan in her hair and then lay panting.

Nate dropped her legs and stretching them out on the bed, she wrapped her arms around his neck and kissed his shoulder.

16

Daisy

After a few moments of lying in silence together, Nate leaned over to kiss Daisy once more before murmuring softly, "I think I might be in love with you."

The words sent electric waves through Daisy's entire being. She smiled up at him and replied, just as softly and just as full of unspoken meaning, "I think I might feel the same way."

"This might sound fast, but I want to marry you," he said after a moment of hesitation.

"Seriously?" she whispered.

Daisy felt like someone had kicked her in the gut. Her opinion of Nate was that he wasn't one for getting engaged quickly, and there he was proposing? While it was what she wanted, it caught her off-guard. This impulsiveness could mean trouble for their relationship. She looked into his eyes, searching for any signs that this was some kind of joke or prank. But all she saw there was love and devotion.

"That's madness," she replied after a moment while struggling to push those thoughts out of her mind.

"I know," he admitted sadly. "I shouldn't have said anything."

"I'll marry you, Nate," she responded warmly, thinking that she would marry this man, no matter how crazy it seemed.

Nate pulled her into a tight hug and kissed her deeply. When he pulled away, she saw his eyes were welling up.

"My mum will want to be there," Nate blurted.

"My mum, too," Daisy said, getting excited about the idea.

"Did you know our mothers were friends until she left the island?"

"No, really?"

"Yeah. When I told her I was in love with Daisy Turner, she cried. She misses your mum and was overjoyed that I'd found a woman to love."

Daisy dipped her head to think, to get all her wishes out. "I want a simple wedding."

"That's okay with me."

"Will you move into the cottage?"

"Absolutely. I'd be happy to wake up not smelling engine oil."

Daisy let out a belly laugh and threw her head back. "Oh God, are we doing this?" she screeched.

"Yep. Shit."

"What's wrong?"

"I need a ring, and I didn't really propose."

"I don't care about anything like that. I'd be happy with a plain wedding band. I don't want fancy jewellery."

"I'll visit Mrs Diamond at her jewellery shop tomorrow and pick one out."

Daisy grinned at him.

She was going to be Mrs Hill.

Luke will be furious she's getting married before him and Freya.

"Can we get married at the Turner Chapel?"

"If you can swing it without your aunt getting involved," he said.

"I'm sure I can keep this under the radar and keep her out of it."

"Whatever you want, Daisy. Just turn up," he said.

"I promise I will."

17

Daisy

It was the end of another week. The movie was wrapping up, and Daisy thought it was the best time to break the two pieces of news to her brothers.

Telling them about her mother would be the hardest, so she planned to tell them that first and then she would tell them about her impending marriage in a couple of weeks.

Erica had finished her scenes and was now relaxing and taking care of Isobel.

Daisy called them to the kitchens on Saturday morning. There was no one staying in Edward Hall, so there were no staff bustling about.

As usual, they were sitting on the metal workbenches like birds on a wire, except she was the one facing them. Taking a deep breath, Daisy spoke, her words barely above a whisper, and then she stopped.

Nate took her spot on the row of people sitting opposite her on the workbench. She took a seat on the bench opposite. Daisy had her brothers in front of her, their wives and fiance at their sides. She couldn't help feeling she was about to break up the gang. One look at Nate, and she found the courage to speak.

The smell of freshly baked bread was in the air. No doubt Jason getting ready to feed them a feast. The aroma deterred her for a moment.

She tapped the countertop twice and found her voice.

"There's something I need to tell you. Something I've been keeping to myself for a long time," Daisy said.

"We're all accepting, Daisy, if you're going to tell us you're a lesbian," Jason said.

Daisy gave him a soft smile wishing it was as straightforward as that. Nate's chuckle drew their attention, and they dismissed that idea as a group.

Archer's brow furrowed with concern, and he leaned forward. "What is it? You can tell us anything. You know that."

Daisy closed her eyes briefly, gathering the courage to continue. "I've been in touch with Mum," she said finally, her voice barely audible.

When she opened her eyes, she looked down the row. Jaws slackened, eyes widened in shock, and then there was a burst of questions from everyone but Nate.

"What?"

That was Jason

"How?" Luke shouted his question.

"When? How long? What the fuck?" All of those were Archer's questions.

No one moved.

Daisy noticed the women stayed quiet, offering silence and sympathy with their expressions. But none of them moved to her. They stayed with their husbands and fiance.

Never had she felt more on the outside than right then. Nate moved to her side and held her hand. She wanted to tell her second piece of news, but her brothers wouldn't let her off easily.

"You need to explain yourself, Daisy," Archer said, using his no-nonsense tone.

Daisy nodded, tears streaming down her face now. "I've been in her life since I was two. I know I should've told you all, but Dad and Mum said it was better this way."

"You've been in contact with our mum for twenty-eight years? And Dad knew? That's a hell of a fucking secret, Daisy."

It was Luke who shot out the questions.

He was off the bench, staring her down.

Nate smoothly stood in front of Daisy, facing Luke head-on. She dropped her head to his back and held onto his hips, fisting his jumper in her hands.

"Easy, Luke. It took her a lot to do this today. Remember one of the questions I asked you in the pub? Go easy."

"Why do you care all of a sudden?" he barked.

"Someone has to," Nate roared at him.

Daisy steeled herself and looked around Nate's stone-like body. He stood like nothing was going to get to her.

Luke took a step back. Freya came to his side and pulled him away and back to the bench.

"Look at you all with your judgement. Cynthia Turner will be so proud of the way you've behaved. Well done, congratulations."

Sarcasm dripped off his words, and Daisy held back a sob. She wouldn't have told them if she knew they would react that way. But Nate had counselled her that to get her memories out, to rid her mind that history would repeat itself, she needed to unburden her secrets.

Not for a secret did she regret taking Nate's advice, but the reality was hard to swallow.

Archer pulled his hand away from Erica's, his face contorted with anger.

"Dad knew," he said brokenly. "He didn't tell us, but he told you?"

She could hear his feelings of betrayal, not just from her but from a father he loved and respected.

Taking a deep breath, Daisy began to speak, her voice barely above a whisper. "Mum can explain it better than me. She has told me pieces over the years, but I tune out every time she broaches the subject. I'd rather not know. I told myself it would be better that way, but now I'm learning, with Nate's help, better out than in."

Archer's expression turned serious as he leaned in, giving Daisy his full attention. "What is it? What about Mum? Why did she abandon us?"

Daisy hesitated, her heart racing. "Cynthia was poisoning her."

Archer's eyes widened in shock, his grip tightening around the edge of the bench.

"What? Daisy, how could you keep something like that from all of us?" Jason said.

Heidi held him back from approaching.

"I didn't mean to," Daisy replied, tears streaming down her face. "I was just so lonely, and she was the only one who understood. She's always been there for me."

Archer stood up, releasing Erica's hand. "I can't believe you just said you were lonely. You had all of us."

"Not really. I just had to get on with things. You all left one by one, and I was on my own in that awful house at the hands of Cynthia."

Luke winced and looked away. She kept her gaze on him.

"You had it out with Jennifer on the lawns, and it brought back memories of something she did to me. I don't know what it is yet. Do any of you know?"

She saw a sea of blank faces. They all shook their heads one by one.

"I was so lonely," Daisy repeated, pleading with them.

"That's no excuse. You betrayed us," Archer replied.

"You think I betrayed you?"

All three of her brothers nodded.

She gasped in shock.

"You've known her your whole life," Jason said. "You didn't give us a chance to have the same luxury."

"You should have told us, Daisy," Luke said. "I can't even look at you."

"It wasn't up to me to tell you," she said through her sobs.

"You've lied for so long. You could have told us after Dad died," Luke said.

"Would you have had a different reaction to what you're having now?"

"Probably not. You're not the sister I thought you were," Archer said.

Daisy felt her heart shatter. Luke still couldn't look at her. Jason was visibly seething with anger. All they were hearing was that she betrayed them, not that their mother was nearly killed by their aunt.

"I need space from you," Luke said and yanked Freya's hand to leave the kitchen.

Daisy watched them leave. Freya looked over her shoulder with a face of sympathy, but she still left. Jason and Heidi did the same. Which left Archer and Erica.

"So that's it? I'm kicked out of the circle, just like she was," Daisy said, finding her anger.

Nate hugged her tight as she spoke to her big brother. The person who said he would be there no matter what.

Archer didn't say anything.

"I'll go. I don't know how long it will take for you to get another accountant. I'll ask Warren if he'll step in for the interim. I'm sure you'll have no objections as he's your personal accountant, Erica."

Erica stared and nodded but didn't say anything. The tears tracking down her face said enough.

"Let's go," Archer said and clasped Erica's hand.

Erica didn't want to leave and tried to stand her ground, but in the end, she left with her husband. As soon as the door closed, Daisy howled into Nate's chest as he held her tighter.

"They'll come around," he whispered into her hair.

"They won't. They've made their decision."

Nate sighed as Daisy's body trembled in his arms.

"Tighter," she whispered.

Nate banded his arms around her, and she burrowed in as much as she could.

"They don't understand how much they're hurting you," he said, his voice low and soothing. "But I do. And I will not let you go through this alone."

Daisy looked up at him, her eyes red and puffy from crying. "What are we going to do?"

Nate pulled her closer, his hands running through her hair. "We're going to stick together. You and me. We'll create our own circle, one that's filled with love and acceptance, not judgement and exclusion."

Daisy's heart swelled with gratitude for Nate. She knew he was the only person who truly understood her and loved her unconditionally. As they stood there, holding each other, she knew they could face anything as long as he was with her.

"We're getting married next week. Your mother is going to be on the island. We'll see what happens then. I think we should stay at my place for a few days. Give you space from your brothers."

Daisy nodded, wiping away her tears. "Okay. I just need some time to process everything."

Nate leaned down and kissed her forehead. "I'll do everything in my power to make you happy, Daisy. I promise."

Daisy smiled weakly at him. "I know you will. I love you."

"I love you too," Nate said, his voice filled with emotion.

They left Edward Hall's kitchen and headed towards her buggy. It was a beautiful evening, the sky painted with shades of pink and orange. But Daisy couldn't appreciate the beauty of it. Her heart was heavy with sadness and hurt.

As they drove to Nate's place, Daisy couldn't help but feel like she was losing a part of herself. Her brothers had always been there for her through thick and thin. And now, they were pushing her away.

But as Nate held her hand and whispered sweet nothings in her ear, she realised she wasn't losing everything.

She still had him.
She still had her mum.

18

Daisy

Daisy followed Nate to the side entrance of his apartment. There were wooden steps leading up the side of the workshop and up to a door. The square glass on the top half of the door was in darkness. Nate fumbled with his keys, found the right one and slipped it into the lock. He turned the key and pushed the door open, and then he leaned in and flipped the switch.

"I wasn't expecting company, so it might look like a college dorm."

Daisy stepped over the threshold after Nate and closed the door behind her. The room was all male, but it was neat as a pin. It was one large room that stretched over the workshop. In the far corner was a door she presumed was the bathroom. His double bed in the far corner was in darkness but was made and had two cushions balanced on top of the pillows.

"This is lovely," she said, walking over to the long sofa in front of a wide-screen TV mounted on the wall.

Nate chuckled. "I can tell you're not impressed. I'm more of a simple guy, Daisy. I don't need much to be happy."

"I'm not judging," she said, taking a seat on the sofa. "It's just that I'm used to seeing places with a lot of decor and personal touches. But you're right, this is really cosy."

Nate sat down beside her, their bodies almost touching. "I'm glad you like it. Can I get you something to drink?"

"Water?"

Nate got up and walked over to a fridge in the kitchen area, grabbed a bottle of water, and returned to hand it to Daisy. As she took a sip, she couldn't help feeling Nate was her hero standing up to her brothers.

His dark hair was messy, and his grey eyes sparkled with love in the dim light.

Daisy wanted to forget that her brothers had walked out and not let her explain. She had to get to work the following day early, so staying with Nate was comforting, but she needed to confront them at some stage.

If they wanted her out, they needed to tell her. Until then, she'd carry on with Edward Hall accounts but get in contact with Warren for him to take over.

Nate sat on the sofa and took a swig of his water. Daisy watched him as he drank, admiring the way his adam's apple bobbed up and down with each swallow. She found herself leaning closer to him, her body almost touching his. Nate noticed her proximity and turned to face her, his stormy grey eyes locking onto hers. There was a moment of silence as they stared at each other, the tension between them palpable.

Suddenly, Nate leaned in and pressed his lips to hers.

Daisy was on him in a flash, needing to feel something other than abandonment.

Their tongues danced together in a sensual tango as Nate's hand snaked its way up her thigh. Daisy moaned into his mouth as he squeezed her thigh, her body coming alive with desire.

"Let's go to bed," Nate suggested. "Let me take your mind off what you said and didn't get to say to your brothers."

Daisy felt a rush of heat spreading through her body as Nate's hand moved higher up her thigh. She leaned into him, her lips never leaving his, as he stood up and pulled her with him. Nate led her towards the bed, his hands roaming over her body as they walked. Daisy was lost in the moment, her mind consumed by the desire she felt for him. When they reached the bed, Nate pulled her close and kissed her deeply once more, his hands undressing her as they explored her body.

Daisy was drowning in the sensations, her mind consumed by the pleasure she was feeling and nothing else. Every touch, every kiss sent shivers down her spine as Nate drove her higher and higher towards ecstasy. She felt his lips move down her neck, his hands exploring her breasts as he continued to drive her wild with desire. Daisy moaned softly, her body arching towards him as she reached the edge of pleasure.

Nate sensed her need and gently pushed her onto the bed, planting soft kisses. She panted as he took one of her nipples in his mouth, sucking gently. Nate's lips on her body were driving her wild, her body trembling with desire. She wanted him inside of her, wanted to feel the pleasure he was creating deep inside of her.

Daisy reached out with her hand, pulling Nate closer to her. She felt him respond by moving his lips lower down her body, his mouth finding her clit. Daisy gasped as his tongue flicked her clit, her back arching up off the bed. Nate gently parted her thighs wider, letting his tongue probe deeper. Daisy cried out as Nate continued to suck, nibble and kiss her pussy lips. She felt her body tense as the pleasure increased. As if Nate sensed her on the edge and pulled away, then he climbed between her thighs.

Daisy moaned softly as she felt his cock head nudge against her pussy. She reached down, guiding him inside of her.

Nate groaned as he penetrated her, his cock slowly sliding into her wetness. He felt her pussy walls tighten around him immediately. Nate gripped her hips and thrust inside her harder, his cock sliding deeper and deeper into her wetness.

Daisy gasped as she felt him hit the end of her, his cock sliding in and out, bringing her to the edge of pleasure. She gripped the covers, her body arching towards him as he penetrated her.

She felt the sensations overwhelm her, her body tensing as she neared the edge. Then Nate pulled out of her, taking her by surprise. She looked up at him and saw him smiling. Then he slid off the bed and knelt in front of her.

Nate used his hands to part her thighs gently as he kissed the inside of her thigh. Daisy moaned softly as she felt his hands spreading her thighs apart. Nate planted soft kisses on her thigh, his fingers gently opening her wet pussy lips. Then he explored her with his fingers, pressing gently against her inner walls.

Her body shuddered as Nate's fingers explored her, bringing her higher and higher towards orgasm. He sucked on her clit, his tongue darting in and out.

Daisy felt her body tense, her breathing becoming more

laboured as she was close to an orgasm. Nate sucked harder, and Daisy's fingers flailed against the bed covers as she lost control. She screamed out as Nate sent her crashing over the edge, her whole body shivering with pleasure as her orgasm tore through her. Then he was thrusting inside her with his cock to ride out her orgasm. Pumping as he stared down at her. She grasped her breasts as they swayed with his aggressive movements, but he pushed her hands away and grabbed her, pinching her nipples. Ripple after ripple turned into an intense throb as her second orgasm loomed.

Nate continued to fuck her, prolonging her pleasure as she rode the waves of ecstasy. Daisy felt her orgasm subside, and she moaned softly, begging Nate to come. Nate pulled out, teasing her with his cock, his tip teasing her clit.

She groaned, spreading her thighs further apart, desperate to feel his cock back inside of her. He teased her for a little longer, easing his cock inside of her just an inch. Then he pulled out, leaving her yearning for more.

"You need to come too," she said.

"I will, but I enjoy giving you orgasms."

Daisy moaned and pleaded with him, begging him to enter her again. Nate teased her for a little longer, then slid back inside her. He slid deeper, and Daisy's fingers gripped the bed covers as she felt her pussy walls gripping his cock. Nate thrust into her a few times, then slid in and out, his cock gliding in and out of her wetness.

She writhed on the bed, her hips lifting to meet his every thrust as Nate fucked her faster and faster. He slid in and out of her, slamming his cock into her.

Daisy felt his cock head brushing against her end as he thrust into her, sending pleasure radiating through her body. She gasped as she felt herself once again approaching the edge of orgasm, her whole body shuddering with pleasure.

Nate's thrusts became quicker with less finesse. She felt her orgasm well up inside of her, the pleasure building higher and higher. Suddenly Nate's body tensed, and she felt him shudder, her pussy walls tightening on his cock as he came. She sighed as she felt his warmth fill up her pussy, her own orgasm intensified as wave after wave of pleasure crashed over her.

Daisy cried out as the pleasure erupted through her body at the same time Nate's cock throbbed inside of her. She gripped his arms tightly, her body arching up towards him as her pussy walls squeezed his cock.

Daisy felt him slide away from her and climb onto the bed beside her. She curled up next to him, her head resting on his chest, breathing heavily.

The two of them lay there for a moment, entwined in each other's arms.

After a few minutes, Nate moved from their cocoon.

"Are you okay?" Nate asked.

"I'm a little lightheaded," Daisy admitted.

"I'll get you a glass of water," Nate said.

As he moved to leave the bed, he kissed her softly on the lips.

Daisy smiled as she watched him leave the bed.

∽

THE FOLLOWING MORNING, Daisy dressed quickly when it was still dark. She tiptoed into the bathroom to make herself presentable and then came back out. Nate was waiting for her in his boxers and a mug of coffee in his hand.

"Here, drink this while I get a quick shower, and I'll drive you up in the buggy."

"You don't need to do that," Daisy protested.

"I know, still going to do it. We're a team now. I understand you have a job to do, a commitment to Edward Hall and I can't camp out in your office and do my boat work. But I will be with you when it's possible. No one is going to hurt you again."

"Nate," she said and sobbed.

Nate put the coffee mug on the counter and was across the room in a flash.

He wrapped his muscular arms around Daisy and held her tightly. She clung to him, burying her face in his chest and letting out gut-wrenching sobs. Nate stroked her hair, whispering soothing words in her ear, and waited for her to calm down.

When she finally pulled away, her eyes were red and puffy. She looked up at Nate, her gaze full of gratitude and vulnerability.

"Thank you," she whispered. "I am so over crying."

"You cry all you want, sweetheart."

Nate brushed her hair away from her face and cupped her cheek. He leaned in, his lips brushing hers in a tender, hesitant kiss. Daisy responded eagerly, her arms winding around his neck as they deepened the kiss for a beat.

"You drink the coffee, and I'll take a shower," he said and kissed her forehead.

While he walked away, she walked to the counter and took a sip of the coffee. She wanted sugar in it. Looking around the countertop, there was none to be seen. Looking in the cupboards, she couldn't find any there either. There was a door she hadn't noticed the previous night, and she headed that way. When she opened the door, she saw it was a walk-in store cupboard with dry goods. She stepped in to rummage for some sugar. As she got to the shelves, it grew darker and then completely dark.

The door clicked shut.

Daisy froze.

She stumbled to where she thought the light switch was, only to knock over tins. Daisy tried the other side and felt along the wall but no light. She was starting to panic. Flashes of when she was a kid came to the forefront of her mind. She was a little girl hammering on the door to be let out, screaming at the top of her lungs. Her brothers were with their dad on a boating trip, and Maggie was supposed to be looking after her, but she got sick, and Cynthia looked after her instead.

Daisy slumped to the floor with her head in her hands. She calmed down enough not to zone out and tried the handle, but it didn't move. Daisy hammered on the door with the flat of her hand every other second. She couldn't hear the shower in the cupboard, so she kept going until he came for her. It was five minutes until that happened. Light burst into the room, and she looked up at Nate's handsome face.

"What happened in here?" he asked, bringing her to her feet..

"I got locked in and then had another episode."

"Oh God, I'm so sorry."

Daisy's eyes watered, and she sniffled, but tears didn't spill over.

She was done crying.

"It's okay, Nate. I know why I'm having them now. It was Cynthia. She locked me in my playroom when I was eight, and the boys were away with our dad. She fed me boiled onions. I've never liked onions, and now I know why."

"Jesus, Daisy. That woman is mad. It's a wonder any of you escaped unscathed."

She smelled the sharp, fresh smell of the soap he used in the shower as she took a deep, cleansing breath.

"I don't think any of us escaped without some mental issues, but we seem to be finding a support system. Even though they've abandoned me. No one hangs around very long."

"I will. I will hang around forever, Daisy. Just like Erica with Archer, Heidi with Jason and Freya with Luke. I will be at your side."

Daisy's hands were cold from the cupboard. She slipped them under his t-shirt and got a gasp from Nate.

"If you do that when we're in bed, I'm buying you mittens," Nate said.

Daisy laughed. "I'm not usually this cold, only after an episode. Hopefully, they'll go away now that I've understood what I'd buried."

"Why didn't you tell anyone?"

"I don't know. I think she threatened me with splitting me up with my brothers or something like that. I don't remember that bit, and I don't think it's important."

"Let's get you to the cottage. Can I stay with you tonight?"

"Looking to cash in a bath token?"

"Maybe..."

He hugged her tightly and then led her back to the coffee cooling on the side. She sipped, looking at him as he laced up his boots. Daisy watched him walk across the open space and pack a holdall that looked like clothing for a few days. She didn't care. He could move in now. Or until Archer kicked her out of the cottage.

Nate dropped her off at the end of the row of cottages. It

was still dark. She urged him to drive the buggy back as she would not leave the Turner estate until she saw him again. He jumped back in and drove away, waving his hand in the air. She chuckled as dawn arrived and wrapped her arms around her body as she walked down the pathway to her cottage. Archer's house was alight, no doubt giving Isobel a feed, but her other brother's cottages were in darkness. She let herself in and headed for the shower. She had a lot of work to get done if they were going to fire her.

Knowing Archer, he wouldn't waste any time, and she expected him to be in her office sometime during that day.

If she could get Warren on a call, she would bring him up to speed on all things Edward Hall.

19

Daisy

For three mornings, she had stayed in bed a little longer, not wanting to face the day. Three days where she hadn't heard from any of her brothers. She carried on with her work, and Warren would arrive soon. He told her he was playing go-between and had talked to Archer.

He left her in the dark as to what they said or agreed. Daisy understood, reading between the lines, that if Warren was coming, she would go. What she didn't know was if that meant she didn't have a home either. She loved her cottage and hoped to make it her home with Nate and any children they might have.

Like he could hear her thoughts, Nate pulled her back to his body, wrapping an arm around her waist. She lifted her knees to her chest as Nate pushed his thighs against hers. She could feel every inch of him.

"Time to go to work," he whispered into her hair.

His warmth comforted her, and she didn't want to let him go. But duty called, and she had to face the music, eventually. Daisy slowly pulled away from Nate's embrace and got out of bed. She could feel the icy breeze creeping in from the window, but she didn't want to close it. She needed to feel alive, and the chill in the air was a reminder that she was still there and breathing.

Nate watched her with concern etched on his face. "Are you sure you're okay?" he asked.

Daisy turned around and smiled at him. "I'm fine. I just need to get dressed and face the day."

Nate nodded but didn't look convinced. "Do you want me to come with you?" he offered.

Daisy shook her head. "No, it's okay. I need to just get on with my day and hope they'll come around. If they don't, then they don't."

Nate turned her by the waist until she was facing him. Their bodies were naked.

"Just remember, I'm here for you. Always."

Daisy leaned into his touch and closed her eyes as he kissed her forehead.

"Five days until I'm Mrs Hill. Either we're living here, or we're living at the workshop. I don't much care right now so long as you're with me."

"I'll be with you," he promised.

Daisy got dressed and headed out of the cottage. The chilly wind whipped around her, making her shiver. She pulled her jacket tighter around her body and trudged towards Edward Hall.

Her mind was filled with thoughts about her brothers and the uncertain future that lay ahead of her. She was so lost in her thoughts that she didn't notice Teddy wasn't bounding out to escort her to work.

She looked to Archer's cottage and saw all the lights were off. No barking or sight of the dog.

"I guess even the dog is angry with me," she muttered.

Daisy felt a sense of comfort in Nate's words. She knew he was always there for her, no matter what. She had thought the same about her brothers, but they showed their true colours. As she entered her workplace, she could feel the stares of her colleagues on her. She knew they had heard about the situation with her brothers, but she didn't let it faze her. Daisy went about her work as usual, putting on a brave face even though her heart was aching.

It wasn't until she received a call from Warren that she realised her brothers weren't willing to compromise. He confirmed he would take over the accounts.

That gutted her.

Halfway through the day, she heard a rap on the door. She knew it wasn't Nate as he was out on a client's boat testing it out. Plus, he would come via her window.

Her brothers had disappeared into thin air. She heard a rap on the door, it opened, and something was pushed through before shutting it again. Teddy rushed to her side and licked her hand. She scooted down and gave him a rub all over and then did it again.

"I've missed you, Teddy," she told the dog.

Teddy gave her a bark and licked her hand again.

The door opened a second time, and something else was sent in, closely followed by the door closing. She heard a screech and a gurgle.

"Isobel," Daisy said and sighed.

She was off her seat and around her desk in seconds,

grinning down at her niece in her wheelie bouncer. Isobel clutched a white piece of paper with writing on it.

"What have we got here?" she asked Isobel.

Leaning down, Daisy lifted Isobel out of the bouncer and cuddled her close, raining kisses over her face and getting more giggles from the little girl. Teddy weaved in and out of her legs in dog excitement.

"I missed my baby cuddles," she said to Isobel and breathed in her baby smells. "You're so cute."

When Teddy settled under her desk, she walked with Isobel to the office door and pulled it open. Erica, Heidi and Freya held hands on the opposite side of the corridor. Her first thought was, why weren't they at work.

Daisy's heart skipped a beat as she looked at the trio standing across the corridor.

Erica, Heidi, and Freya entered the office, and Teddy ran to them, wagging his tail. Daisy placed Isobel in her bouncer and went back to her desk to get the white piece of paper.

Daisy furrowed her brows and looked at the piece of paper in her hand. It was a hand-drawn picture of a unicorn with a rainbow mane and a smiley face. She let out a chuckle and handed it to Isobel, who held it up and gurgled with delight.

"Hey girls, what brings you here?" Daisy asked as she ushered them into her office.

Erica, Heidi, and Freya exchanged glances, and then Erica spoke up. "We just needed a break from work and thought we could hang out with our favourite Turner.

"Christ. If I'm your favourite Turner, things must be bad."

The girls laughed and settled into her seats. Erica sat on the low window sill with Isobel bouncing around the room.

"I appreciate the visit and the baby and dog love, but I don't want you taking sides on this. You have to live with my brothers. They don't want to know me."

"We're working on that. We want to hear your side, plus we're women sticking together. So I'll decide whose side I'm taking, not my husband," Erica said.

"Absolutely," Heidi nodded.

"I've only just got to know you, Daisy, and I know you're a good person. Our husbands should be the first to understand whatever reason prompted this situation. They had their dad to help them through their teenage years and become the men they are. I bet Freddie will be turning in his grave at their behaviour."

Daisy smiled at them and gestured towards the coffee machine.

"You know, you could have just called me, and we could have met for lunch or something. But it's good to see you all here."

She leaned back in her chair and looked at her three sisters-in-law. They were all dressed in casual clothes, which was unusual for them since they all had jobs.

"Why aren't you at work?"

"Inset day," Freya said.

"The film has wrapped," Erica said.

"Day off. I love mid-week days off," Heidi said.

"Jason said he'd stopped making you breakfast. I can assure you that will resume tomorrow," Heidi declared.

She hauled up a box and plonked it on the desk. When she peeled back the lid, Daisy eyed up the cupcakes. They were lemon, her favourite.

"I'm working on Archer," Erica said.

"I think Luke is more pissed off you're dating Nate Hill than anything else," Freya said.

"Listen, I know it's tough with the guys right now, but don't let them get to you. You're a strong woman, and you'll get through this," Erica said.

Daisy felt a lump form in her throat, and tears pricked at her eyes. "Thank you, Erica. That means a lot to me."

"Anytime," Erica said before taking a cupcake.

Daisy chuckled and reached for a cupcake. "Well, that's Luke's problem, not mine. I'm happy with Nate, and that's all that matters."

"Will you tell us about your mum?" Erica urged.

Daisy couldn't help but feel grateful for their support. She sat back in her desk chair and nibbled on the cupcake.

"I don't know when it became normal or how it was orchestrated, but I knew my mum all along when my brothers thought she'd disappeared. I thought they would guess when she was the next-door neighbour. I've never seen a picture of my mum, and there were none in Turner Hall. She told me she looked completely different after a makeover. The older I got, the more information my mum told me. I rarely saw my mum and dad together, but when I did, they were marriage goals right there. Imelda, my mum, was dealt a shitting deal in life, and it was crunch time when she moved off the island. Her parents and Freddie were in on it, and no one else knew. They purchased two houses in Imelda's dad's name next door to each other in Northern Scotland."

"Pete Boyle, right?" Heidi said.

"Yeah, the butcher. His wife knew too. They were terrified at what was happening to Imelda when Freddie was away. Eventually, Freddie had no choice but to send her away. My mum said she tried to fight it but confessed that she would be dead if she hadn't moved off the island."

"Why?" Erica asked.

"Because Cynthia was poisoning her. It wasn't in the food. Maggie's mum, Melly, was cook then, and she didn't allow anyone near her food. Plus, the Turners never ventured downstairs, apart from Imelda and Freddie. Then the four of us when mum left."

"Oh bloody hell. How was she poisoned?" Freya asked.

"We're not entirely sure, but after what Luke said, I think I know for sure it was the plant pesticide. Mum said Freddie had insisted she only drank and ate from plates and cups he personally washed, and they kept them in their rooms at Turner Hall. When that happened, she rallied, but if she ate from Turner crockery, then she became ill. When Dad was away, she spent a lot of time at her parent's place during the day. She wasn't permitted to stay over, there was no plausible reason on a small island, and us kids had to be in bed early. I was six months old."

"Why was she being poisoned?"

Daisy could smell the yummy goodness of the cupcakes and leaned over to take a second one. The women followed suit. Eric broke off a tiny piece and handed it to Isobel.

"That I don't know. I think my mum suspects, but she never said anything."

"There are so many secrets coming to light. Where is your mum now?" Freya asked.

"In Scotland, still at the house. I keep asking her to move back to the island and live in the fifth cottage. But now, with the boys acting like they are, I'm not so sure now."

"It will turn out fine. They'll get over this with our help, and you'll be back to playing cards on the giant table in no time."

"A bit cold for that," Heidi muttered.

"You know what I mean. I miss you at dinner," Erica

said. "Isobel misses you, and Teddy goes bonkers every morning when you pass, and he isn't allowed out."

"That's cruel," Freya said.

"Archer's being an ass. If Teddy comes with Daisy to work, then he would have to come into this office to get him. He's too steaming mad at the moment to see right."

20

Daisy

Daisy shuffled into her dining room, flipped open the lid of her laptop, and shuffled back to her kitchen. She flipped the switch on the kettle and waited for it to come to a boil. The conversation called for tea. Coffee wasn't anywhere near as comforting.

While the kettle was coming to a boil, she opened the cabinet in front of her and stared at the mugs. Different sizes for different hot beverages. She needed a bucket, so she chose the biggest. Dropping two tea bags into the mug, she poured the water while it was still bubbling and let it brew for a couple of minutes. Once she'd got rid of the tea bags, she added some milk. Daisy grabbed the biscuit barrel, stuffed it under her arm, and then picked up her mug.

She shuffled back to her laptop in the dining room to see her mum waiting for her.

"Hey, Mum," Daisy said when she'd settled down in the seat and hugged her mug.

"Hey, sweetheart. Are you still in your dressing gown?" she asked, moving her head around the screen to get a better look.

"Yeah. Not feeling the need to get dressed right now."

"And you're drinking tea. The next thing you're going to do is dip a chocolate digestive into the tea."

Daisy smiled at her mum, then dipped her head and concentrated on making sure the biscuit didn't get too soggy and plop into the tea. She gave her mum a side-eye glance and ate the soft biscuit.

"Things must be bad. Tell your mum all about it."

"They hate me," Daisy said once she'd finished her biscuit.

"Who do?"

"My brothers."

"Still?"

Daisy dropped her head and hummed. She had told her mum the truth as soon as it happened. She needed to be warned. All her brothers had Imelda's number, but only as a next-door neighbour. Someone who would water the plants to collect a parcel for them.

"Have you had any messages from them?" Daisy asked.

"No. But then I wouldn't expect them to get over it anytime soon."

Daisy put her head in her hands and willed herself not to cry.

"I know they didn't take the news well, but they'll come around. Freddie raised good sons," her mum coaxed on the other end of the video call.

Daisy grabbed the box of tissues from the side table and blew her nose.

She shook her head and then looked at her mum with watery eyes.

"No. They were so angry with me."

"We talked about this, but I have to admit I didn't think they would walk away from you."

"It's all gone horribly wrong. I thought I could be happy here. Make a life, fall in love, get married—"

"Hey, did I hear you upset?" Nate said from the entrance to the dining room.

He was out of shot but could see the laptop screen. Nate gave an eek face and went to step back.

"Is that him?" Imelda asked, grinning.

"Yeah, do you want to meet him?" Daisy said, a smile splitting her face.

"Better had if you're going to marry him in a few days," Imelda replied. "The last time I saw him, he was a baby."

Nate rolled his eyes and then smiled. He ran his fingers through his hair and then turned to the picture hanging on the wall. Daisy watched as he tried to make himself presentable. She couldn't care what he looked like, but straight out of bed was his best look.

"Come and meet my mum," Daisy said and reached her hand out to him.

Nate walked over and stood behind Daisy, then bent to kiss her cheek and wrap his arms around her neck. Daisy instantly felt better and draped her arms over his.

"Hi, Mrs Turner," Nate said and waved with one of his hands.

"Hi, Nate. I knew your mother," Imelda said with a sad smile.

"Yeah, she said she knew you too. She said you were great friends before you had to leave. She thinks the same thing the rest of the island thinks. I haven't told her anything."

"I appreciate that, Nate. I'll tell her some of it when I see her at the ceremony. Does she know I'm coming?"

"No. I've not said anything. Mum and Dad think they're going to be witnesses with Maggie and Bailey."

"Good. It will be easier if no one knows, then there is less pressure on them to keep it a secret. I hope to be gone before anyone gets wind that I'm on the island."

"I understand. I think she'll be thrilled to see you."

"I'll be happy to see her too."

Daisy leaned to the side, looked up at Nate, and stared at him. He gazed back down at her and kissed her head.

"I'm going to make a coffee, then get a shower. I need to get to the workshop."

"No problem, I have a few bits to do. I'll meet you back here or at the workshop?"

"Here," he said and then kissed her lips.

It was brief, but it warmed her to her toes.

"Later," he said and then strode off the kitchen.

"I can tell you two are in love," Imelda said when Daisy looked back at the screen.

"You don't think it's quick?"

"It was quick with your dad. I knew within days of meeting Freddie that I wanted to marry him, despite him being a Turner. I don't regret a single day with him or when we were apart."

"Wasn't only seeing him three days every six weeks hard?"

"I think I saw him more than army wives see their husbands. They can go a year and not see their husbands. I may not have seen him for long, but we made it count. It was the cards the universe dealt us, and we made the most of it."

"It makes me sad," Daisy said. "It's all such a mess, and I don't think Archer, Jason and Luke will ever forgive me."

"They should be angry at me, not you. I think they forget that you're the youngest, even though you're probably the most put together, the smartest and the most adult out of all of you kids."

"Thanks, Mum, but I don't feel very put together. In fact, I feel like I could fall apart. If it wasn't for Nate, I would wallow or run away."

"Then I'm glad you met him when you did. Seems fate had her plans for you."

"I am so looking forward to hugging you. I can't believe I'm only going to see you for an hour."

"Cynthia might be eighty, but I wouldn't put anything past her. I don't want to risk anything for you or the boys. Maggie will help you with whatever you need that I can't sort out for you."

"She's been so lovely."

"She cherished you when you were a newborn. I had to prise you away when you were nursing, then as soon as you had your fill, she had you in her arms straight away."

"Am I mad marrying him?"

"What does your heart say?"

"He's the one," Daisy replied immediately.

"Then it doesn't matter what anyone else says. He knows you could get kicked off the Turner Estate, he knows you might end up living above the workshop, and he doesn't care. You both have oil under your finger nails, and it doesn't deter either of you."

"I miss you, Mum."

"I miss you too, sweetheart."

"Maybe you'll sneak back again soon?"

"Maybe," Imelda said with a watery smile.

"I'll let you go. See you in a few days," Daisy said, grinning.

"I'll be the one in the ridiculously over-the-top hat."

"Awesome," Daisy said and put her palm on the screen.

Her mum did the same, and they said their goodbyes.

When the screen went back to the default setting for the video call software, Daisy felt the loss immediately.

Sighing, she drank her lukewarm tea and then shuffled back to the kitchen to make a coffee. There was a three-hour shift ahead of her on the financial helpline, and then she had Edward Hall work to complete. Warren was due to arrive the Monday after the wedding, and she wanted everything perfect so she could walk away with a clean slate.

21

Daisy

The frosty air greeted her the following morning. She needed to be at her desk early, so there was no time to languish in bed next to Nate's warm body and watch the sun rise over the lawns.

She kissed Nate goodbye in bed and then walked through her house to the back door. Nate had a spare key, so she locked up as she left and trudged down the path in chunky lace-up boots and thick socks. She had her corduroy skirt and roll-neck jumper to keep her warm in her office. The woollen coat was an added layer until she reached her sanctuary.

When she shouldered her way in, the lights were off, and there was nothing on her desk. Jason was still pissed off with her. Heidi was wrong about when breakfast would resume.

"Fuck this," Daisy said out loud.

She wanted porridge, and if her brother denied her

breakfast, she would go to Maggie.

Daisy turned on her heel, marched out of Edward Hall, and breathed in deeply to approach Turner Hall kitchens. She was careful to circle the house from the front and not the back to avoid Cynthia's rooms and the morning room. It would be the first time she had entered Turner Hall without her brothers beside her. They had no idea why she wouldn't step foot in the place, and she wasn't about to enlighten them now they had shown their true colours.

When she approached the outside white wooden stable-style door to the kitchens, she peered through the window to see if Maggie was in there and to make sure her brothers weren't. When she only saw Maggie and Bailey with a cup and saucer in their hands standing by the stove, she turned the handle and walked in.

Maggie turned to see who had come in and beamed at Daisy. Daisy felt the smile warm her all over. Maggie was the next best thing if she couldn't have her mum.

"Come here, child and give me a cuddle," Maggie said after putting her cup and saucer down. She opened her arms, and Daisy flew into them.

"Hi, Maggie."

"Hello, child. What brings you here this early?"

"Jason won't feed me, and I really miss my morning porridge."

"Sit yourself down. There is some warming on the stove. I'd made a batch for Bailey and me, but there's plenty. Any leftover is for anyone who wants it."

"Are you sure I'm not taking your breakfast?"

"No, we've eaten. Sit down, and I'll bring it over. Do you want tea or coffee?"

"Tea if there is any in the pot."

"There is always tea in the pot, Daisy," Bailey replied like she had wounded his pride.

Daisy grinned at him and shrugged off her coat.

"Why is Jason withholding food?" Maggie asked.

"I broke the news to them about Mum."

Maggie looked to Bailey, and they exchanged a glance.

"He didn't take it well?" Maggie asked as she ladled out a bowl of steaming hot porridge.

"None of them took it well. They're not talking to me. Archer is not letting Teddy come to work with me, Jason isn't providing breakfast, and Luke has disappeared completely. I would make my own breakfast, but I always hoped I'll get to my office, and he would've gotten over that I had a relationship with our mum. They seem to forget they had years with Dad on the rigs when I didn't."

"Give them time. They'll come around," Maggie said.

Everyone was saying the same thing. But Daisy needed a timeline.

"I miss them," she said.

"I bet they miss you too," Bailey chipped in.

"What about the girls?" Maggie asked.

"They came with Isobel to my office to tell me they are supporting me and working on their stubborn husbands."

"Do they know about the wedding?"

Daisy shook her head.

"No. Why should I tell them I'm getting married when they won't hear me out about Mum? I don't want their sullen faces, and I don't want to put the girls in an awkward position."

"Well, Bailey and I will be there. I am so looking forward to seeing Imelda. It's been too long since I last hugged her."

"I bet there will be tears all round. You'll have one set of grandparents there. I'm sure they're going to be overjoyed to see their daughter too," Daisy said.

Bailey placed a mug of tea in front of her. She handed him her travel mug, and he gave her a wide smile and went to fill it up for her.

"They will be happy to witness their youngest grandchild get married."

"It will be the quietest wedding ceremony I've ever been to. Me and Nate, his parents, my grandparents and you two and my mum. That's it."

"Are you sad about that?"

"Not really. I want to be married to Nate. I want to start a life with him, a family. When Warren arrives to take over the Edward Hall accounts, then I will be jobless."

Bailey came over and placed the travel mug of tea by her side. "You know there are no accountants on Copper Island. All the business send their accounts to the mainland," Bailey said.

"Really?" Daisy replied.

She thought back to Nate's call to the hotline and wondered where they got their advice from.

"When one door closes, another opens," Bailey said.

Daisy didn't feel quite so dejected at the prospect of being jobless. There was potential if she was completely shunned.

22

Nate

Nate revved the engine of his motorcycle and pulled away from the curb, the roar of its power echoing along the empty dirt road. He glanced over his shoulder at his passenger. Daisy smiled back at him, her face aglow with excitement. It didn't take much for her to agree to a bike ride to test out his restructuring.

He'd gone onto the runway like his dad had suggested making sure it was road worthy and then asked if Daisy wanted to go out. She didn't hesitate to say yes.

It was the night before they were getting married.

"Ready?" he called.

"Always," she shouted back, though the engine nearly drowned her voice out.

He gave her a wink and gunned the engine, sending them careening down the track and up to the Turner Estate, the setting sun casting long shadows in their wake.

Daisy held on tight as they raced along, the wind and

the road beneath them a blur, the surrounding treeline of bare branches.

Each bend in the road brought something new to admire, and each straight way was a chance to sit back and take in the beauty of the passing scenery. He couldn't go as far as he wanted as it was the private land. For his plan, he went somewhere familiar and where he knew he could take the bike.

Nate had been planning this day since he suggested they got married, but there had never been a chance once Daisy's brothers turned their backs. Now, as they sped along, he had only one thought in his mind.

Propose.

Nate knew that when he reached the spot he had chosen, the cliffs above the sea, he would have the perfect setting to ask her to be his wife. Even though they had already agreed and would be in front of the vicar the next day.

As they arrived at the cliffs, the sun had all but set, its dying rays painting the sky a deep pink. Nate stopped the motorcycle and took Daisy's hand, squeezing it tightly as he got off.

"Come," he said, leading her to the edge.

The cliffs rose steeply above the sea, their jagged edges silhouetted against the twilight sky. Nate and Daisy stood at the brink, looking out in awe at the majestic landscape.

Nate stepped forward and scooped Daisy into his arms, spinning her around and kissing her deeply. When he finally put her down, he reached into his pocket and produced a small, velvet-covered box.

"Daisy," he said, his voice wavering with emotion, "I've known you only a couple of months, and we're getting married tomorrow. But in that short time, I've grown to love you more than I ever thought possible. A girl needs a proposal, so will you do me the honour of turning up tomorrow and becoming my wife?"

He opened the box to reveal a sparkling diamond ring, his grandmother's ring. Daisy gasped in delight as she saw it. Nate remembered she said she just wanted a wedding band, but he wanted more for her.

"Yes!" she said, her eyes bright with tears. "Yes, Nate, I will turn up tomorrow!"

Nate slid the ring onto her finger, then kissed her again, this time with even more passion than before. They stood there, holding each other tightly, until the last of the light had faded completely. As they turned and made their way back to the motorcycle, Daisy smiled at him, her eyes twinkling with excitement.

"We must be mad," she said.

Nate smiled back. "We can be mad for the rest of our lives," he answered.

23

Daisy

*D*aisy awoke on her wedding day with a thrill of anticipation. She hadn't slept much, her mind too overflowing with excitement for Nate and the day to come. She rolled out of bed, feet already padding across the carpet to her bathroom before her eyes had even opened.

Nate stayed at the workshop even though they'd spent every night together since they'd first slept together.

She smiled at the old-fashioned tradition, thinking she would be Mrs Hill in a few hours. Reverend Wendy Sprite would meet them at Copper Island church. They'd toyed with marrying in the Turner Chapel, but Daisy didn't want to risk her mother being spotted by her brothers or her Aunt Cynthia.

It was a chilly day in early December, but the sun shone brightly through the window, and the sky was painted blue for a beautiful day.

Daisy hummed as she descended the stairs to her

kitchen and filled the kettle. Nothing would take the smile off her face that day. As she leaned against the countertop, scrolling mindlessly through her social media, waiting for the kettle to boil, her attention was directed to the tapping on the glass.

She looked up at her back door and almost dropped her phone. Daisy put the phone down, lifted her robe and ran to the back door. She flipped the lock and swung the door open.

"Mum," she said and sobbed. "I thought you were coming later."

"You're worth the risk, Daisy. I took an earlier boat. Mum and Dad met me at the boat, and we had breakfast. They'll meet us at the church. Have you had breakfast?"

"No, I'm too nervous."

"You must eat, even if it's a piece of toast. Have you got any peanut butter?"

"Yeah," Daisy said, grinning. "I'm so happy you're here."

Daisy grabbed her mum and hugged her hard. The bonus of her brothers not talking to her was that there was no danger of them being interrupted. Still, she wasn't going to risk sitting out on the back patio. Her mother made her breakfast while she dashed upstairs to have a shower. When she came back downstairs, a feast awaited her in the dining room.

"That is not peanut butter on toast," Daisy said, pointing to the scrambled egg, bacon, toast, coffee and orange juice spread. "I didn't have half of those ingredients in my fridge."

"No, but Maggie did. She snuck in and made this for you. She wanted to make you your pre-wedding breakfast so we could have some mum-and-daughter time."

"I love Maggie."

"Me too. She writes amazing letters about you all. I feel like I have been with you for the last twelve months."

Daisy's shoulders sagged, and she shuffled to the table.

"It does look good," she relented.

They tucked into their food and chatted and laughed about nothing in particular. It was soon time to get ready. Daisy hadn't thought about how she would get to the church undetected and now was in a panic in her bedroom.

"Mum!" she shouted down the stairs.

Her mum came racing up the stairs and skidded into the bathroom, looking like she was about to fight a bear if need be.

"What's wrong?"

"How am I going to get to the church in a wedding dress and no one see me and instantly know what's going on?"

"Oh, sweetheart. It's winter time. You've got that long black wool coat. That will cover your dress, and I can take your veil, and we can put that on when we get there."

Daisy let out a puff of air. "Right, okay. Crisis averted. Will you help me into my dress?"

"I want nothing more. This is everything I dreamed it would be. Just you and me on your wedding day, giving you away. I wish your dad was here."

"Don't make me cry, Mum. You'll spoil my makeup."

Daisy stepped into her flowing gown of white. A thousand tiny pearls seemed to dance around her as the fabric floated around her feet like a willow in the breeze. She smiled, her heart alight with joy and anticipation for what the day would bring.

Daisy studied her reflection in the mirror, her eyes dancing with joy. She was happy, and she felt it right down to her bones. Daisy would soon be a married woman. It wouldn't matter what her brothers or her aunt did. She would have Nate by her side. Daisy wondered if that was how her mum felt when she married her dad. Them against the world.

Her mind drifted to Nate, the man she was going to marry. He had such a gentle soul and a kind heart. She thought of the way he had taken care of her that first time she had an episode. He didn't shy away or think she was weird.

Somehow she knew they were meant to be together, and today was the day they would become man and wife.

She moved through the house, her steps light as she checked her clutch bag. They would come straight back to the cottage after the ceremony. Her mum would get on the next boat leaving the harbour, and Daisy's grandparents would go back to the butcher's, so it didn't attract any attention. Maggie and Bailey would go back to Turner Hall like nothing had happened.

Finally, she stepped out into the sunshine, breathing in the crisp fresh air.

"Let's do this, Mum. Can you drive?"

"I will be your chauffeur with pleasure, but I think it would be best if Bailey drove you. I'll take the back path to the church across the graveyard."

Bailey cleared his throat at the end of the pathway.

"Good morning, Miss Turner. You have a beautiful day for it," he said in his low baritone voice.

"Hi, Bailey. Thank you for driving me."

"It will be my pleasure. Even though I think these buggies are death traps."

Maggie laughed behind him and took her mum's arm, and they hurried off out of sight. There was an advantage to being the end cottage. To get to the church, she didn't have to pass her brother's cottages.

"I've parked the buggy at the other end. We'll nip through those trees so we don't pass the other cottages."

"Good thinking Bailey. Let's go. I don't want Nate to think I'm not coming."

"Absolutely."

Nate was waiting for her at the church. His parents were in the front row. Nate was ready to receive her as his bride. Daisy's heart raced as she thought of the moment when they would finally be together, the look of love and devotion in his eyes when he caught sight of her.

The minutes ticked by, and Daisy felt her excitement growing. She couldn't believe she was about to start a new life with the man she loved.

Butterflies fluttered in her stomach as she stepped into the vestibule. Imelda was there, ready to affix her veil. Bailey took her coat, and then Daisy turned to look at her mother.

She burst out laughing.

"How did you get that hat here undetected?"

"Stealth, Daisy. I'm the mother of the bride, and it's my duty to wear a big hat."

"You look fabulous," Daisy said and clutched her hand.

Daisy stepped forward to the wooden door that would take her inside the church. Her eyes were wide, and her heart was pounding with anticipation. Daisy took a deep breath and walked through the doors.

She saw Nate standing at the end of the aisle, his eyes meeting hers. Time and space seemed to melt away as the two of them locked eyes. Daisy felt a wave of emotion wash over her, and tears welled in her eyes. Imelda hooked her arm through Daisy's arm and walked her down the short aisle where she handed Daisy over to Nate.

"You look sensational in a suit," Daisy said, her voice all breathy.

"I love your dress, but I can't wait to get you out of it," he whispered, leaning down to kiss her cheek.

Nate extended his arm, and Daisy stepped forwards, allowing him to pull her close. Daisy felt the warmth of his embrace and knew that she was home. They held each other for what felt like an eternity until the officiant cleared his throat and asked them to turn and face each other.

She and Nate spoke their vows with all the love and commitment they felt for each other, their eyes never leaving each other's faces. When Reverend Sprite declared them husband and wife, there were cheers and tears of joy from those gathered.

As they turned to walk down the aisle, Daisy and Nate's gazes met, and they shared a knowing smile. They would never forget the day.

They stepped out into the sunshine, now Mr and Mrs Hill. Daisy smiled, her heart lighter than ever. They had made it, and now their life together could begin.

The day was everything Daisy had dreamed it would be. Cynthia Turner hadn't spoiled it.

Nate drove Daisy back to the cottage when everyone scattered to their homes.

Daisy felt the gentle warmth of Nate's arm around her shoulder, and she felt more content and at peace than ever. She and Nate were husband and wife, and that was all that mattered.

From then on, their life together would begin. With or without her brothers in her life.

24

Nate

"Are you sure you don't want another?" Nate said as he kissed the inside of Daisy's thigh.

"Have we slept?" she answered lazily in the dark.

"There might have been a twenty-minute snooze, but I'm not sure."

"Mr Hill?" Daisy asked.

He could hear the smile in her voice, and he loved that. They'd been married for less than a day, and she sounded as content as he felt.

"Yes, Mrs Hill."

"Will you open the curtains?"

"It's dark, babe," he whispered as he kissed the apex of her thighs.

"Just the ones on the left. The others can stay closed."

He felt her shudder, and then she canted her hips towards his mouth.

"Orgasm or curtains?"

"Curtains and then an orgasm, please," she said and laughed when he grunted and rolled away.

He'd do anything she asked, and he would do that for the rest of their lives. It was madness that they had married so fast, but he felt it in his bones that she was the one for him. His parents bearing witness as well Daisy's mum sneaking onto the island to walk her down the aisle, was all he needed as support that he was not mad and neither was she.

Nate left her warm legs to army roll off the bed, and he landed on his feet. He strode across to the curtains and flung them open. He looked across the lawn to the tree line and could see a hint of pink through the bare branches.

Nate assumed they must have slept as the sun didn't rise until half seven in December. He walked back to the bed, put a knee on the mattress and then circled Daisy's ankles with his hands and pulled her to the edge. The apex of her thighs brushed against his knee.

"Oh," Daisy murmured.

She lifted her hips and brushed again. Nate could feel his knee getting damp with her arousal.

"You want to come this way? Are you sure you don't want something else there?"

"You've turned me into a crazy person craving these highs."

"I'll be happy to deliver, Mrs Hill."

He leaned forward, put his fists on the mattress, and covered her body with his. Then he rolled them with her on top. Nate reached over and put the lamp on so he could see her.

"You have fantastic breasts," he said, cupping them and toying with her nipples until they hardened.

Nate looked up at the woman sitting astride him and

raised his hips so she'd get the hint. She closed her eyes and dropped her hands to his cock to position him, and then she sank down. Their groans filled the room. The feeling of sliding inside his wife was nothing he had ever expected to feel. The sense of belonging so wholly to another person drove him halfway to orgasm. To know she was his forever was enough to tighten his balls and for him to drop a hand to press his thumb to her clit. She rode him painfully slowly, her eyes still closed, and now a hand cupping the breast he'd left unattended to hurry her to ecstasy. He pushed up, and she dropped down and then felt the now familiar clench around his cock that Daisy was nearly there. He grabbed her hips with both hands and stilled her movement so he could power up and take them both to oblivion. She was panting above him. Her hands were flat on his chest as she arched her back and called out.

"Nate," she shouted.

His name called out as an expletive was all it took for him to find his release. Pulse after pulse from him. Daisy's seemed to last minutes as he kept thrusting and keeping her in position. Once her thigh muscles relaxed, he did an ab curl to sit up and hug her to his chest, kissing her neck and whispering her name.

"This is how I want to wake up every morning," Nate said.

"You won't get any argument from me. I've never felt so at home than in your arms."

Nate held back his sob. He felt the same way. If she was in his arms, then all was right in his world.

"I love you," Daisy whispered as she looked out the window.

The section she was staring at was floor-to-ceiling glass with sash fastenings. Nate fell back onto the mattress, still hugging his wife. He settled her at his side, pulled her thigh over his legs and her arm across his stomach. Nate made sure her head was on his chest, and she could see out of the window.

The morning after they were husband and wife, they watched the sunrise and the frost twinkle on the lawns. He grabbed the blankets and pulled them up so they were cocooned.

"Are you happy?" he asked as he stroked her hair back from her face and down her back.

"I've never been happier."

That was good enough for him.

25

Daisy

The sun shone brightly that day on the quayside. Daisy was sitting on a tea chest, kicking her legs against the wooden panel and slurping her coffee. She clutched her travel cup like a lifeline, terrified that her brothers were going to show up.

She was waiting for Warren to arrive. They'd arranged to meet at the warehouse. Erica had assured her that Archer, Jason and Luke were interviewing all day for the new conference and banqueting manager.

Warren had arrived on the island two days ago and had settled himself into her office. He'd spent the first day meeting with Erica to go over her accounts. The second day Warren had updated her, he'd spoken with her brothers for a way forward that would be seamless to the business. All of this was done via phone because she didn't want him in her home. It would be better if he didn't know she'd gotten married. Her brothers should know first.

Warren appeared irritated that he couldn't see her, but she was still in honeymoon bliss five days after the ceremony.

She didn't like that her brothers weren't asking her to stay, but she accepted their decision. Warren was gentle when he told her.

Erica sat on the tea chest next to her and huddled into her coat as the wind blew in off the Atlantic.

"Still not used to Copper Island breezes?" Daisy asked as she bit into her apple.

"Honey, this is not a breeze but a gale. The wind is going to cut me in half," she complained, frowning at the sky.

"Try standing on an oil rig," Daisy quipped and grinned at her.

"I keep forgetting you're a bad ass," she said, nudging her shoulder.

"I'm not really."

"You are. I can only imagine what it was like being the only woman on that rig."

"I had my brothers to protect me."

"You did, and you'll get them back," Erica said.

"I'm not so sure about that. Warren is making himself comfy in my office."

"He is?" Erica said. "Why is he in there?"

"Warren told me he spent the afternoon with you in there going over your accounts."

Erica stilled and then looked at Daisy. She took her hand and squeezed.

"Honey, I only review my accounts when I absolutely have to once a year, and January is not the month I look at them. I don't leave things to the last minute."

"But it's next month you have to pay your taxes."

"I pay my taxes immediately. Warren's firm does my

accounting straight away. I don't wait until the last minute. They were filed last June and paid the same month."

Daisy's breathing came fast, and she rubbed her chest. "Why did he lie to me?"

"I wonder if he's lying about anything else?" Erica said.

"Who's lying?" Heidi asked as she sat on the tea chest on Daisy's other side.

"Warren. He said he spent time with Erica going over her personal accounts. He said he was holed up with my brothers to see a way forward without me," Daisy said.

"What?" Heidi said. "There is no way Jason would've had time. He's been planning menus for our next group. They have special diets. He's also been interviewing, and then he's been with me because I want a baby."

"Aww, really?" Daisy said and gave her a hug.

"Yeah. So Warren hasn't been plotting your demise with your brothers. They may be pissed at you but don't want you out."

"Who wants you out?" Freya said, joining them and edging herself in between Daisy and Erica.

"I thought my brothers did, but it seems Warren has been telling fibs."

"Maybe he's in love with you?" Erica said.

"He's missed that boat," Daisy muttered. "I'm off the market."

"Has Nate proposed?" Freya asked.

"I think he's already done that," Heidi said, lifting Daisy's left hand. "Why are you wearing an engagement ring and a wedding band?"

All three women were staring her down with broad smiles.

"Umm... Oh look, there's Warren. I want an explanation," Daisy said and jumped off the tea chest.

"Daisy," Erica called after her. "Who walked you down the aisle?"

"My mum," Daisy shouted back, and she heard a collective audible sigh.

Daisy marched over to where Warren was approaching. He was all smiles until he clocked her expression. She hoped it was set to fury.

"Hey Daisy, I'm not late, am I?" he asked, pulling up his coat sleeve to check his watch.

"Why did you lie to me?"

"Lied about what?"

"About seeing my brothers, about seeing Erica in my office. I've had to work on a teeny tiny screen in my cottage because you were hogging the large monitor in my office."

"I can explain…" he said, wincing.

But Warren didn't say anything.

"I'm waiting."

"Well, you lied to me," he huffed. "Why didn't you say anything about why your brothers weren't talking to you?"

Daisy was wide-eyed. The man had coached her, trained her and made sure she had all the knowledge she needed to run Edward Hall accounts, but she didn't answer to him. She certainly didn't owe him any information about her private life.

"What?" she snapped.

Warren was getting red in the face. He folded his arms across his chest, bent at the waist and leaned in. He didn't whisper.

He yelled.

"Why didn't you tell me you were in contact with your mother? Why didn't you tell me you knew where she lived? You should have told me you met with her recently."

Daisy took a step back. Everything was closing in, and

she couldn't hear what he was saying or anyone else because the blood rushing around her head was drowning everything out. Another flashback, and this time, it was in full technicolour. She was in the playroom with her toys and the yellow armchair hugging her rabbit toy. Her Aunt Cynthia was towering over her, arms folded and yelling at her.

Are you in contact with your mother? When was the last time you saw her? Do you know where she lives?

She remembered crying and running to the radiator under the window of her playroom and sitting on the floor with her arms wrapped around her knees and her face hidden from Cynthia's gaze.

It was enough to bring her back to the present. Just in time to see Nate punch Warren in the face. Daisy scuttled back to the girls, and they embraced her in a cuddle.

"Are you okay, Daisy?" Erica asked.

"Yeah, I'm okay," she answered, not taking her eyes off Warren and Nate.

"How did Nate get here?" Daisy asked.

"He has all our numbers, and we have his. He insisted that if you spaced out, even for a minute, we were to send him an SOS. And here he is," Heidi said.

She sounded utterly delighted with Nate.

"Why did Nate punch him?"

"I think because he triggered you."

Warren got a punch in, a blow to Nate's cheek, but Nate barely moved. They were the same size, but Nate hauled boat equipment around all day, and Warren sat behind a desk.

"You're seeing this Neanderthal? He has oil under his nails," Warren said. "You're just a prick tease."

A collective gasp went around the girls.

Nate wasted no time and punched Warren hard. Warren fell to the ground clutching his jaw.

"That's my wife you're calling a prick tease, you piece of shit," Nate said through gritted teeth. "I should throw you in the dock water for a comment like that."

"Married? As if... what the fuck does she see in you?" Warren growled.

Daisy left the cocoon of the girls and took a step forward, waiting for Nate to say something.

"Is it wrong that this is hot, two men fighting over a woman they're in love with?" Heidi said.

"No," Freya answered.

"Absolutely not," Erica added. "This is totally filmworthy."

Daisy walked to where Warren was lying on the floor and lifted her hand with her wedding band.

"Take a close look Warren. I have oil under my nails. Oil still stains my hands from working on the oil rigs. I don't think it will ever go. And you know what? I don't care. Why did you lie to me?"

"I love you Daisy. I thought you loved me. I thought that was why you wanted me to come to the island to rescue you from your small life here. I was going to take you away."

"I didn't want to leave. You made me think my brothers didn't want me."

"You told me they didn't want you," he countered. "I just didn't correct you because I hadn't seen them."

Daisy looked at Nate, who was glaring at Warren and then back at the girls, who were arm in arm, all grinning at the scene.

"Go home, Warren. Get off the island. You've done enough damage."

"But I love you, Daisy Turner," he said emphatically.

"It's Daisy Hill," Daisy replied and threaded her fingers into Nate's hand and dragged him away from where Warren sat on his arse on the quayside.

Once they were a few feet away, Daisy faced Nate, went up on her tiptoes and kissed him.

He returned the kiss, deeper, more passionate and lifted her off the ground. He kept her in his arms when he leaned back.

"You taste like a thunderstorm," he said.

"Aww," one of the girls said and sniffed.

Daisy turned her head to Heidi, who was wiping away her tears.

"Are you pregnant?" Daisy asked, remembering how Erica was when she was pregnant.

"Maybe," she said, sniffing as tears dripped down her face. "That is the most romantic line I've heard anyone say."

Daisy wriggled out of Nate's arms, much to his amusement, and she ran over to Heidi to give her a cuddle.

"I'm going to be an aunty again," Daisy sang.

"You are, but not for like seven months," Heidi said and grinned at the girls.

"Hey," Nate said gently.

Daisy moved away and went to her husband.

"Are you okay?" he asked.

"Yeah," she said, smiling.

"What happened?"

"He was yelling at me about Mum. It was the same kind of questions Aunt Cynthia was yelling at me on those days she locked me away. She was trying to find out where my Mum was living. I wouldn't have known at the time she was living up in Scotland. Mum always met me on the mainland straight off the boat."

"So you weren't able to give her any information?"

Daisy shook her head. "I remember just crying for two days every time she came in the room. I never thought she was going to let me out."

Nate wrapped her in his arms, and she buried her face in his jumper. He wasn't wearing a coat in the icy wind but was still warm enough to keep her snug.

"I got to get back to work," Nate called over her head to the girls.

"We're not going anywhere," Erica called out.

"You want to come with me or stay here?"

"I think I'll stay here. They'll have questions about you being my husband."

Nate laughed. "All right. I'll see you at home for dinner."

"You will."

Nate kissed her soundly, sweeping into her mouth for a tongue touch and then left her standing on the dockside dazed but for entirely different reasons.

"You married him," Heidi stated.

"Yeah," Daisy replied, watching him saunter down the quayside.

She watched his arse move until he was out of sight.

"Freya has gone to get coffee. We need details and, if possible, a picture of the dress," Erica said.

"I can do that," Daisy replied, hugging them both.

26

Daisy

*D*aisy brought Nate to Turner Hall kitchens to get breakfast. It was to fortify herself to meet with her brothers in Edward Hall kitchens. They now knew Warren had played her, that she was married, and that she was led to believe they no longer wanted to know her. The girls had reassured her that was not the case, but it didn't stop her from having a sleepless night.

"Are you sure it's all right to be here?" Nate said, looking up at Turner Hall ominously.

"Of course, Maggie and Bailey only saw you for a few minutes after the wedding, so it will be a relaxed way to get to know them."

They ducked in through the door and shook off the snow from their coats on the threshold before removing them and hanging them up on the new rack Bailey had nailed to the wall. He mumbled and muttered about constant traffic and needed the kitchen to be tidy and not have all their coats slung over the nearest piece of furniture. He'd even brought down special hangers to hook onto the fastenings so it didn't ruin the *line of the coat*.

That got him an eye-roll. Daisy had laughed and reminded him that she and her brothers had worked where no one cared about the drape of a coat.

He replied he would teach them.

Daisy smiled at the conversation. Bailey always took care of them in any way he could.

"Hey Maggie, what's cooking?" Daisy said, and she crossed the flagstone floor to where Maggie was at the kitchen sink.

"Oh, Daisy, how lovely to see you. I'll cook you whatever you want. Nate, come and sit down. Let me know what you want to eat."

"I don't mind whatever is to hand," he said and came across to sit on the bench seat at the old country-style kitchen table.

"That's not how it works around here, Nathaniel," Bailey said in his deep voice and unsmiling face.

Nate blanched and looked to Daisy for help. Maggie intervened.

"Oh, don't mind Bailey, that's his happy voice," Maggie said, waving at him.

Bailey moved to their coats and re hung them while Daisy and Nate settled at the table. Daisy immediately got up and made them a coffee.

"Do you want me to make a pot of tea?" Daisy asked Maggie.

"Oh yes, I could do with a cuppa. What brings you here this morning?"

"I'm meeting my brothers for a pow-wow, and I'm terrified. Nate's coming with me for moral support and to kick anyone's ass if they're mean to me."

"I'll come over with you. I have to drop some dishes over to Jason. It will break the ice a bit if I make conversation first."

"I love you, Maggie," Daisy said.

"I love you too, darling girl. Now what am I making?"

"Porridge for me if you have it on the go, or if not, then I'll have a big fat bacon bap."

Nate gave her a side glance and laughed.

"I'll have the same at Daisy, although I'm veering towards the bacon bap."

"No problem. I'll get it made, and then we can go across."

"I'm going upstairs, Maggie. Do you need me to do anything?" Bailey asked.

"No, we're all set down here. She's had her breakfast," Maggie said and rolled her eyes.

"Nice to see you, Nathaniel. I hope you're not a stranger to this kitchen. You're welcome any time, with or without Daisy," Bailey said.

"Thank you, Bailey," Nate replied.

Bailey nodded and went through the archway, and ascended the stairs. When he was out of sight, Nate turned to Daisy.

"Why does he call me Nathaniel?"

"He's old-fashioned. It's taken us a while to get him to use our first names and not call us Mr or Miss Turner," Daisy said.

"Oh, right. Then I'm glad he didn't call me Mr Hill. I'd be looking for my dad."

Maggie and Daisy chuckled.

"There isn't a thing that man wouldn't do for me. Just

because I'm a Hill and not a Turner, makes no difference. That kindness now extends to you."

Nate leaned in and kissed her cheek.

"It's going to go fine with your brothers," he said.

"I hope so. I'm so wired I think I might cry."

Daisy let Nate and Maggie settle her nerves, and then she stuffed her face with Maggie's food. They were soon wrapped up again and trudging across the snow-covered grass to Edward Hall. Maggie entered first, followed by Daisy, and then Nate came in last and pulled the door closed.

Daisy stopped when she saw the girls on one stainless steel table and her brothers on the other one opposite. They played catch with one of Isobel's toys. Isobel was busy bouncing in her wheelie chair and watching the action with her alert eyes.

"Hey," Daisy said.

She could happily throw up at the situation.

"Oh, Daisy, come over here. We need reinforcements. Nate, you're on the boys' team," Erica said, pointing to the seat next to Luke.

"Actually, how old are you?" Heidi asked. "We sit in age order around here."

"I'm younger than Luke," Nate answered.

"And Daisy," Freya replied and cackled.

"Really?" Erica said and gave Daisy an exaggerated wink. "Nice work."

Daisy was relieved that the tension was broken but talking about her marrying a younger man, albeit two years, was not what she wanted her brothers to hear.

"All right, kids. I need to get back to the kitchen. Jason, here are the dishes I borrowed last week. They're cleaner than when you gave them to me," she said, giving him a stern look.

"Thanks, Maggie. I'll have a word with pot wash," Jason replied and grinned.

"You do that," she said, giving him an adoring smile like he could do no wrong. "I've fed Daisy and Nate, so you're off the hook for today, but it might be a good idea to resume your breakfast skills for tomorrow."

"I've already made plans, Maggie. Don't worry."

Jason looked straight at Daisy, and her heart pounded. Did Jason's look signify forgiveness?

"Don't I get a hug?" Archer asked after hopping down and opening his arms wide.

Daisy flew across the kitchen and jumped into his arms, letting out a loud sob.

"Hey, Daiz, it's all right."

"Will you ever forgive me?"

"I think it's us that need forgiving," he said.

He let her down so she could stand, and she swiped at her eyes to get rid of the steady stream of tears.

"I've missed you all so much this past year, and when I got to live here permanently and then lose you all broke me apart," she said.

"But had you had Nate, right?" Jason said while he gave her a cuddle.

"Yeah," she said and looked over to Nate, who was cuddling Isobel, making faces at her.

Daisy's heart melted at the scene, and she wanted more than ever to have kids with him.

"Right, we all made up?" Luke asked as he wedged in to hug Daisy. She wrapped her arms around his neck and held on tight.

"Yeah, I think so," Daisy said.

"Okay, well, now that you're back, you need to help with

finding my replacement because no one we've interviewed can organise shit," Luke said.

"And you think I'll find someone?"

"We're hoping so," Archer said. "There has to be someone on the island that wants to work for us."

"I'll see what I can do, but no promises. Those numbers don't crunch by themselves. We may want to look at the mainland. We don't have a good rep," Daisy replied, hopping up onto the stainless steel bench. Everyone took their places, and for once, Daisy had someone to her right. She looked up and saw Nate cuddling Isobel.

"You look good holding a baby," she whispered.

"We can start immediately," he whispered back and kissed her cheek.

Freya sat to her left and passed her the cupcake box. "They're to die for. I think he puts cocaine in them. They are so addictive."

"I've missed these too," Daisy said.

"I told you they'd come around, honey," Freya whispered.

"Yeah, I know. I just didn't see how it would happen. But then Warren's lies didn't help."

"I fired him," Erica said further up the row.

"What?" Daisy said and leaned forward.

"Yep, no one hurts my family and gets to benefit from me. He's out, and so is the firm. So, um, I'm kinda looking for an accountant," Erica said and gave Daisy an eek face.

"Anyone else need me to fix their problems?" she called out and laughed.

The row laughed and dug into their cupcakes. They passed Isobel up the row to Erica, who nursed her while they chatted. Jason looked at the interior door to the kitchen. They could hear footsteps. Then a rattle on the doorknob before it swung open. They all leaned forward. There were no staff due in, and they were all there.

"If it's Stan and his fucking spanners, I'm running out the other door," Luke said.

They didn't have to wait long when a woman walked through the open door carrying two archive boxes.

"Oh my God, Mum," Daisy said.

She jumped off the metal bench and ran to her mum. She wrapped her arms around her waist and buried her face in her neck.

"It's so good to see you. How did you manage to avoid being seen?"

"I don't care about being seen. I've been doing some thinking, and Cynthia Turner doesn't get to bully me any more. I missed Archer and Jason's wedding. I had to sneak in to see yours. I want to be there for Luke and Freya's wedding day. So I'm here," she declared.

Daisy looked back to her brothers and their partners. None of them showed anger, but they were pensive, to say the least. Isobel let out a string of unintelligible words and wriggled in Erica's lap.

"You want to meet Granny?" Erica whispered into Isobel's hair.

Isobel let out a noise and wriggled again.

"I think that's a yes," Archer said, picking up his daughter.

He walked to Imelda, leaned in and kissed his mother's cheek. "Meet your granddaughter," he said quietly.

Daisy clamped her hand over her mouth to stop the wail begging to come out.

"She's beautiful," Imelda said.

"You won't get any argument from me. What's in the boxes?"

"They're from your dad, in case Cynthia made your life difficult after he died and you came back to run the place. From what Daisy has been telling me, I think now's the time I told you all the truth."

"How long are you staying?" Daisy asked.

"As long as I'm welcome. I have brought my own food, though," Imelda quipped.

The rest of the group laughed, but Daisy's eyes widened. "That's not funny, Mum."

"Sure it is. I'm feeling optimistic."

"I have no idea why you're pissed, Daisy," Jason said. "But if Mum wants to have her own food, then it's not a problem."

"I am kidding. I thought it was amusing. Looks like it's too soon for Daisy."

"It'll be way too soon for these guys when you tell them too," Daisy said and then turned to Jason. "Let's see if you're all smiles then."

Daisy huffed and folded her arms over her chest, feeling like she would throw a tantrum. But then she remembered she might be the youngest of her siblings but still the most mature.

"All right. Why don't we go back to mine? I made a whole batch of chilli for us to eat after we made friends with our sister. So one more and a bunch of boxes will make it more fun," Jason said.

"Well, there are a dozen more on the other side of the door. If we all took one, and the guys took two, could we get them across?" Imelda asked, looking hopeful.

"How much did he sneak out of this place?" Archer asked.

"All the important stuff. But he wrote a lot of it out too. All his diaries are in there. He wrote diaries from a really young age and never shared them with anyone. He hid them in my bedroom to prevent discovery.

"Have you read them?" Jason asked.

"Yeah. They were dispatched with me when I left the island, and then as he filled each one, we left them at my house in Scotland. Far away from Cynthia's paranoid prying eyes."

"Right. Good job, we all have the day off," Archer said. "Let's go and get settled in."

Daisy moved to where Nate was and wrapped her arms around his waist, looking up and resting her chin on his chest.

"Still glad you married me?"

"Never been surer, Daisy. I can't see my life ever being boring. I never had siblings, so to have three brothers-in-law and their wives and fiancé is crazy mad with the noise and the banter, but I'm really happy."

"Not just because you love my bath?"

"Not just because of the bath, no," he teased.

Nate quickly kissed her and then helped her with her coat.

"Come on, let's go hear the bombshells," Daisy said.

27

Daisy

Daisy felt good being in the company of her brothers and the girls. By the time they'd eaten and Isobel had been put down, there wasn't much energy left to plough through history, so they decided to leave the revelations for another day.

Nate held Daisy's hand as they walked the frosty path to their home and approached the back door.

"Give me the keys," Nate said, pressing a kiss to her lips.

"They're in my pocket. Feel free to rummage," she said and grinned at him.

Nate cupped her breasts over her coat and squeezed. She let out a laugh.

"That is not my pocket," she said.

"You said I could rummage," Nate replied as his hands went to her bottom. He hauled her against his body and wrapped her tightly against him.

"Harder," she whispered.

He squeezed her tighter and buried his face in her neck. "This okay?"

"Yeah. I feel safe here," she said.

"Good," he replied, then kissed her neck.

Nate took her keys from her pocket and told her to stay where she was. He flipped on the kitchen light and wedged the door open. Daisy cocked her head, frowning at why he was letting all the cold air in. Then he advanced with a wicked grin. She didn't have a chance to ask what he was doing when he swept her up bridal style and carried her into the house.

"Have you lost your mind?"

"Now that it's official, this will be our home to raise our family. I thought it was best I carried you over the threshold."

"That's so sweet, Nate. Are you sure you want to live here, in the shadows of Turner Hall?"

"Yeah. I've always felt lonely down there on the docks, and I love it up here. It's so peaceful, and you're happiest when you're with your family. It's perfect for both of us."

"I think we should have a bath to celebrate. Then tomorrow, we can move anything you want up from the workshop. We'll borrow Ralph's trailer. It's much bigger than the wheelbarrow."

"Sounds good, beautiful."

"I might even unpack my boxes too."

Nate carried her up the stairs while she pressed her lips to his neck above his scarf. There wasn't much room, but she found his warm skin and marvelled that she would be doing this for the rest of her life.

∽

"We're going to need a bigger table," Bailey said as he frowned at the assembled group.

"And a longer coat rack," Archer quipped.

Everyone had congregated in Maggie's kitchen, much to her delight. She smiled and bustled as she dragged in different-sized tables. Erica placed Isobel on the day bed in the room attached to the kitchen, and she put the baby monitor on the countertop near the coffee machine.

"I'll need to get a few more mugs," Erica said.

They arranged all the tables and the bench seat with mismatched chairs on one side of the tables. Everyone sat in a row in age order, and Daisy clutched onto Nate's thigh. She had someone to her left.

"Oh yes, this works. I'm no longer nearest the kettle," Archer said, nudging his mum with his shoulder.

"You look like birds on a wire," Bailey said.

The chatter was loud, joyful and as argumentative as four siblings, their partners and finally, their mum waited for Maggie to make them breakfast.

"Are you sure I can't help you?" Imelda asked from the end, half getting up.

"Absolutely not. Stay where you are. This is what I do, and I love it. It is so wonderful to have you all here."

Maggie sniffed and pulled out her hanky from her trouser pocket. She wiped away a tear and cleared her throat.

"Right, who wants what?"

"That bloody woman!"

All heads turned to the half-glass wall to see a woman stomping down the stairs and muttering like a mad woman.

"Who's that?" Jason stage whispered.

"One of the nurses your aunt has hired. They don't stay long," Bailey said in a quiet voice, barely moving his lips.

"Oh boy, I can't say she makes a good patient," Heidi said.

"There is not a thing wrong with her. She doesn't need nurses. She needs someone to boss about. Jenny is long gone, and we don't see her," Maggie said.

The nine of them were still fixed, looking at the opening where the woman would enter. When she did, they tilted their heads in sympathy. She was young and close to tears.

"What's wrong, honey?" Heidi asked.

"I took her breakfast up. She asked yesterday for sausages and scrambled eggs."

"That's what I made her," Maggie answered carefully.

"Well, now she's decided she's vegetarian and trusts nothing coming from the butchers."

Imelda let out a howl of laughter. She slapped the table with an open palm and clutched her stomach with her other hand. Maggie got the giggles too, and even Bailey smiled.

When Imelda recovered enough to breathe evenly, she looked at the young nurse and patted the empty chair next to her.

"Sit down, love, have a cup of tea. You cannot imagine how much you have made my day."

The nurse looked puzzled. A row of shrugs moved to her, except for Daisy and Nate. They were smiling. Imelda bent forward and looked down the row to Daisy.

"You have to agree that was a little bit funny."

"I suppose," Daisy replied.

Nate took her hand and linked their fingers.

"It means I'm free. She's on the back foot," Imelda said.

"You're going to tell us what this code talk means, right?" Luke asked, bouncing his stares between Imelda and Daisy.

"After breakfast. We're going to your old rooms and break the cycle for Daisy," Imelda said.

"All right, let's get some food cooking. CeeCee, do you want something to eat?" Maggie asked the nurse.

"Whatever is going will be fine with me. I'll get the teas and coffees," she said.

"I'll do that," Bailey said with a hand on her shoulder. "You deserve a break. Hopefully, with all of us, you'll consider not leaving."

"She's so mean," CeeCee muttered.

"That she is, but she pays well, and this kitchen is a sanctuary. You're welcome here anytime," Maggie said.

"Thank you, Maggie," CeeCee said, sounding brighter than before.

Bailey boiled the kettle and placed the mugs in a row. He put a pot of coffee on while Maggie set the gas burners going and clanged pans and pots on them.

"Full works, right?" Maggie said.

A chorus of agreement went up around the room, and they splintered to separate conversations talking over one another while they waited. Silence fell around the room once they cleared the plates and put the mugs in the dishwasher. CeeCee made her excuses and left them alone.

"Come on, honey. Let's get this over with. You need to see the room, and then your episodes will be over. I promise," Daisy's mum said. "We'll all be there with you."

Daisy immediately looked at Nate.

"Let's exorcise some demons," he said and gave her a quick kiss.

"What shall we do with the tables, Bailey?" Archer asked.

"Leave them there. You might feel like coming back," he said.

"We won't be strangers," Daisy said.

They donned their coats, scarves and gloves. Archer had

Isobel in his arms, and they left via the back door. Bailey stood stoically at the door, holding it open and nodding to all of them as they left. Maggie was to his left in the warm and accepted a kiss and a hug from all of them.

"Oh God, I can feel the evil wafting out of the bricks," Luke said as they circled the perimeter.

Archer had opted not to go up the back stairs, instead going through the front door. He told his siblings that this was their ancestral home, and if they wanted to go in, they wouldn't sneak around. Nine against one was enough to keep Cynthia in her rooms while they roamed. Not that they knew anything important was with their mother. They didn't care about snooping undetected.

Imelda led the way holding Daisy's hand. Nate held her other one, and the rest followed behind like protection detail. Her hands became sweaty, and she tried to pull away, but neither her husband nor her mother would let her go.

At the top of the stairs, they looped back and turned left to walk along the wide corridor. The red patterned carpet didn't meet the skirting board. A thin strip of wood flooring and a gold runner edged the carpet. Nothing else was in the corridor. No paintings or small tables with lamps like there had been when Daisy was a child and teenager.

"Has she stripped everything away?" Jason muttered.

"Maybe. Less dusting," Archer said, ever the practical one.

There were titters behind Daisy, and she gave herself a small smile. Finally, they reached the end of the corridor, and Daisy saw the end room had its door wide open. Then a woman stepped into view.

Imelda pulled her hand from Daisy, raised both palms to her mouth, and pressed them hard. Daisy looked at her mum, who had tears coming down her face.

"Melly?" Imelda said through a sob. "Is that really you?"

"Come here, child," Melly said and opened her arms.

Imelda ran at full pelt to the woman, and she wrapped her in a hug. Both women were crying. Then a sniff sounded to Daisy's side.

Daisy looked and saw Maggie standing there, trying to contain her cries.

"Who is that woman?" Nate asked.

"That's Maggie's mum, Melly. She looked after us when we were kids. She was the cook then, taught Maggie everything she knew," Archer said, coming up and wrapping an arm around Maggie's shoulder and bringing her close.

"I better get Mum back to the chair. She is fit as a fiddle and sharp, but she can't stand for very long," Maggie said and bolted forward to her mum.

"This is like a reunion," Heidi said and wailed.

"Good Lord, are your hormones going to be like this the entire time you're carrying our child?" Jason asked.

Daisy heard an oomph, and she smiled. She knew Heidi had jabbed him in the side, and her brother was exaggerating the hit.

"Do you want to go into the playroom?" Nate asked.

He turned her by her shoulders and kept his hands on them while he dipped his chin and kept eye contact with her.

"Yeah, let's do this," Daisy said.

"Okay, which door?" Nate asked.

"This one," Luke said, pointing to a closed door to their right.

He opened the door and looked in, still keeping his hand on the doorknob.

"There is nothing in here. Bare floorboards. Not even curtains. You should be fine," Luke said.

"Okay," Daisy said, nodding and letting Nate take her into the room. She expected to lose her mind, freeze on the spot and then shake uncontrollably, but with Nate's hand in hers, she felt nothing. Not a thing. Then she glanced at the radiator. The green paint was peeling. She remembered crouching next to it, the armchair to her other side. It was a great hiding spot.

"The chair in your workshop used to be over there," Daisy said, pointing.

"I can get rid of it if it upsets you?" Nate said.

"I think I'm going to be okay. Let's go and join Mum, Melly, and the others," Daisy said.

She dropped Nate's hand to hug him and kiss his cheek. "Thank you for holding my hand."

"Always," he replied and kissed her quickly, aware her brothers were watching her closely.

They left the room and closed the door, seemingly on her past. The group moved to the main room at the end of the hall and found Maggie, Melly and her mum on folding chairs, laughing and holding hands. Imelda looked up and stared at Daisy.

"You okay, sweetheart," Imelda asked.

"Yeah, Mum. I'm good."

"Come and look at this Polaroid. It is the last picture we had taken of us," Imelda said.

Daisy and her brothers stood behind the three women and looked at the picture Imelda was holding.

"I was so tiny," Daisy said.

"Six months old."

"Look at Dad," Jason said. "Archer, you look exactly like him. I can't believe I haven't seen this before."

"It was the week I left the island. I'd forgotten about this photo," Imelda said, stroking Freddie's image.

"You don't look well in the picture," Jason said.

The girls joined them and passed the picture around and laughed at the brothers and how cute they looked.

"We suspected Cynthia was poisoning me, but we couldn't prove it. Freddie made me eat food only Maggie and Melly had prepared but wouldn't let me eat from anything in Turner Hall. I had my own special plates and cutlery. We still don't know what she did or how she did it."

"I think I know one part of that," Luke said, taking the photo. "We found a list of ingredients for plant killer. When we showed it to Ralph, the gardener, he didn't recognise it as something he had made up for Cynthia. Ralph spoke to his Dad, and he said the same, and Ralph's dad took care of all the pesticides on the Turner estate."

"I bet she sprayed the plates somehow. God, I was so ill, but when Freddie was home, I recovered quickly. I don't think she meant to kill me. Just piss me off enough to leave."

"She got her way in the end," Archer said.

"It was that, or we feared she would die," Melly said.

"I didn't, and I'm here," Imelda chirped.

"Why, though?" Daisy asked. "Why did she want you to leave? She couldn't change the will or inheritance, so why go to the trouble of splitting you up?"

"She let slip about going into labour. As far as her father and grandfather were concerned, she turned down the man her grandfather had chosen for her to marry and swore she would never marry."

"She never did marry," Luke said. "We checked."

"Fate had its way of stopping her plans," Imelda said. "She had a child with Jonathan, the man she wanted to marry, but he wouldn't marry her because her father didn't approve of him. If her father didn't approve of him, then Jonathan couldn't live on the island. I think her father knew of a child somehow but couldn't prove it. He had her followed, but no one ever knew she met with Jonathan every school holiday and spent time with her son part-time for short bursts."

"Oh god, how history repeats itself," Archer muttered.

"It was her doing that, that gave me and Freddie the idea. Freddie knew of Jonathan and of her child but never said anything. He, by chance, saw them, and then the idea of the two houses and him staying for a few days with me before he headed back to Copper Island was spawned from her sneaking off-island. He wondered why she went to so much effort to hide her child. But Freddie was safe in the knowledge that her child could never inherit. It's written in the will and rules for Copper Island succession."

"Wow, I wonder if she knows Freddie knew?" Erica said.

"I don't care anymore," Imelda said. "She went to extreme lengths to get you four to come back. But I guess it doesn't matter now. You've all found happiness, had babies or are going to have them. You have a thriving business and live on this beautiful island."

"What do you mean she went to extreme lengths? It was our choice to come back," Archer said.

"Luke. Daisy said you found out that Jonathan and her son Benny are buried under unmarked gravestones."

"Yeah, that's right. It was in the ledgers Mrs Philbott gave us. The tin had the birth certificates."

Imelda laughed. "Oh wow, where was it?"

"In the warehouse. We found it when we were clearing it out."

"That makes me laugh. She turned this house upside down looking for it but wouldn't tell us why."

"It had birth and death certificates and a concoction that we now know was poison."

"Luke, when did they die?" Imelda asked.

"Um, a year ago, I think, maybe eighteen months."

"It was two years ago," Imelda said. "She had to get her ducks in a row for her plan to work."

"What plan?" Daisy asked.

"The rig you worked on was a Turner rig. When Freddie died, I was told that Jonathan still wouldn't marry her or come to the island with Benny. She carried on meeting them. Now that she had the entire inheritance after her father died a year later, the trips were more extravagant. Jonathan had retired from teaching and didn't want to live on Copper Island. Cynthia bought a villa on Lake Como. Apparently, it held a special place in their hearts, and that was where they were when the accident happened that killed Jonathan and Benny."

"How do you know this?" Archer asked.

"I have my sources," Imelda said, winking at her eldest son.

"So she shut down a rig to get us to come home?" Daisy asked, putting the pieces together.

"My guess is that no matter what she thinks or does, everything is about continuing the Turner name and keeping control over Copper Island. If she lives as long as her grandfather, she needs to make sure she lives out her days in the luxury she is used to. Cynthia couldn't run this island for too much longer. She wouldn't have the body and mind to do it."

"That makes sense. The island went drastically downhill when her father died. That would have been about six years ago," Nate said.

"Freddie never told her a word about how to run the island. Her father and grandfather had no plans for her to inherit, but with Freddie dead and Cynthia still living, the will dictated the estate went sideways along the family tree and not down."

"I'm not sure how I feel about all this," Jason said.

"Best not to think about it. You'll burn a hole in your stomach. Make the best of what you have now. Don't dwell on what might have been because you can't control that. You can control what you have now," Nate said.

"Those are wise words," Erica said, bouncing a fussing Isobel.

"I read a lot of books," he replied.

"Have you seen the library here?" Imelda asked.

Nate shook his head.

"Come on, let's go and explore. Bailey gave me his keys," Imelda said, raising a bunch of keys and jangled them.

28

Daisy

Erica, Heidi, and Freya splintered off with Isobel and went back to Jason's cottage, leaving Daisy with her mum and brothers and Nate. Maggie said she would take Melly home after promises of visits from Imelda.

"Where are we going?" Daisy asked as they trotted down the main staircase and across the marble foyer.

"Do you remember skidding across this floor in your socks?" Imelda asked Archer and Jason. "Luke, you were too young and kept falling over, and Daisy, you hadn't been born yet. Your grandfather would get so angry. He was a firm believer in children not appearing in his company until they were at least ten years old."

Archer laughed. "Yeah, I have great memories of messing about when he wasn't home. Then that one time, he was in his study and came out bellowing at us."

"Oh yes, I remember that. I have never run so fast in my

life," Jason said, chuckling. "I'm laughing now, but I was shitting myself he'd catch up with us."

"We just scattered," Archer said. "Dad took Luke and ran out the front door."

"I ran after them, laughing as we jumped down the steps and then down the pathway," Imelda said, slinging an arm around Archer's waist.

"And then we all met up for ice cream," Jason said.

"Man, that was a good day," Archer said and sighed. "I wish we had more of them."

"You'll have memories with your own kids. You're going to have so many campfire legends to tell your grandkids, with all of you living next door to each other. Your kids are going to grow up together, and then they're kids, too," Imelda said.

Daisy wiped away the tears as she listened to stories before she was born. When her mum was happy even though she was living under a tyrant's roof. They walked to the end of the wing on the opposite side from the study, and the morning room was situated. Imelda tried the door handle to see if it was open, and it was.

"Come on, let's show Nate where all the serious books are," Imelda said, furrowing her brows to make her look like an elderly college professor.

Nate laughed and dropped Daisy's hand to move to the library. It was like someone said books, and he ran in that direction.

"Holy shit," he shouted from inside.

Daisy and her brothers were still outside, letting him have the run of the library. When Daisy was younger, she thought they modelled Beauty and the Beast films in her library.

"Are you really happy, Daisy?" Archer asked quietly. "You married really quickly."

"Quicker than you?" she countered with a grin.

"Fair point. But I wouldn't be your big brother if I didn't make sure you're happy with Nate."

"He makes me happy. He takes away my loneliness," she said, and she had three faces look stricken at her. "Don't give me that look. It's hard being the youngest and the smartest."

"You never said anything," Jason said.

"I don't think any of us shared what we went through in this house. I have days where I want to strike a match and burn it to the ground, but this house has too much history. As much as she was awful to all of us, I don't wish her dead. But when the old goat does go, this place needs to be utilised in some way. Obviously, Nate won't let anyone in that library based on how quiet he's gone, but we should come up with something. Maybe a permanent movie set?"

"That's not a bad idea. Maybe we could bid for a series to be filmed here, not just a movie. They used loads of houses on the mainland for period dramas."

"We'll put it on the list," Daisy said.

Imelda came out of the library smiling. "Nate is moving in there, so let's leave him and go to the morning room."

Imelda marched off to the other end of the mansion, and all four of them stayed where they were. It took a full minute for Imelda to realise she was on her own.

"Do we have to?" Luke asked.

"Yes, come on. I'll protect you. She won't be in there, anyway. She knows I know, and she knows I'm spilling all the secrets, so shame will keep her up there in her rooms. Come on," she said and held out her hand.

It wasn't for any one of them, just a simple gesture that she wanted to be their mother. Luke went first, and Daisy wanted to sob for him as he had the rawest deal with Aunt Cynthia besides her. Then Jason followed. Archer snatched up Daisy's hand, and they strode towards their mother.

"I have an idea. Well, it was Bailey's really," Imelda said when they caught up.

Daisy looked to her brothers and then back to Imelda walking away. None of them knew what she meant. Using the bunch of keys Bailey had given her, she unlocked Cynthia's morning room and kept the door wide open. She picked up the nearest heavy thing and wedged the door open.

"No more locked doors," Imelda announced.

They moved as a group to where the conservatory was overflowing with plants. Daisy had only been in that room once as an adult, but it still took her breath away.

Its grandness and grandeur filled the air with a sense of awe and wonder. Her grandfather would recite stories of visitors to the estate filled with admiration and envy of its many features, particularly its exotic plants and blooms.

The conservatory was massive and filled with various plants and flowers, from rare orchids to exotic lilies, from tropical palms to fragrant roses. The walls of the conservatory were adorned with glass, allowing the warm sunlight to pour in and bathe the room in an array of colours. The light reflected off the glass of the walls and filtered through the greenery of the plants, creating a truly magical atmosphere.

The scent of the flowers was intoxicating. The heavy aroma of roses and lilies scented the air, while the delicate aroma of orchids and jasmine wafted around the room. The humid air was filled with the sweet smell of nectar and the alluring aroma of pollen.

It was clear why the manor house conservatory was so popular. It was a place of beauty and serenity where

Cynthia, no doubt, could escape the hustle and bustle of the house and take in the beauty of nature.

"Do you know how rare these flowers are? Back in the 70s, Grandfather Turner used to host a festival of flowers. The islanders were encouraged to grow their own too. Blessed with long summers and higher temperatures, Copper Island can grow so much. But the flowers in this conservatory and the walled garden have flowers from all over the world. Centuries ago, the original Turners encouraged their overseas guests to bring seeds, and then this monstrosity of a conservatory was born."

Imelda was talking like she was giving a guided tour, and in some respect she was, because Daisy didn't know a lot about Turner Hall or its history. Their aunt squirrelled the information away.

"We should resurrect that," Archer said.

"I bet that is why there is so much lavender here. I'm sure the lavender farm Freya loves so much would want to get involved," Luke said.

"There are a lot of flower farms on this small island, but I bet they've cut right back since the tourists don't come anymore."

"We can change that," Daisy said.

29

Nate

"Do you know where the saying, *marry in haste, repent at leisure,* comes from?" Nate asked her.

"Nope. Sounds like something from the Bible."

Nate smiled into the crook of her neck. They were curled up on a giant armchair in the Turner Hall library. He'd fallen in love with the room. Bailey had handed him his personal key so he could come and go when he wanted. Lately, he was in one of three places. The workshop where business was picking up, the cottage or the library.

He had yet to meet Cynthia Turner and hoped she didn't like reading books.

"Have you read the Bible?" he asked, pulling his head away to look at her face.

Daisy was in layers of wool. Her skirts acted as a blanket over them. Her sloppy roll-neck jumper was loose enough for him to snake his hand up and cup her breast while he read.

"Not entirely. Growing up, we had to attend Church on Sundays and listen to Father Sheldon's sermons, but I wouldn't say I knew a lot about the Bible. Certainly not enough to know one psalm from another."

"Hmm, well, it's not from the Bible. It's from a play written in the late 1600s."

"Is that what you're reading now?"

"Yeah."

"Are you making a point?"

Nate hummed aloud. He was nervous that Daisy would change her mind about her hasty marriage now that her memories had surfaced and she could stop fearing Turner Hall, Cynthia Turner and her past.

"I'm scared I'll lose you, that you'll ask for a divorce," he whispered.

Daisy moved so quickly, dropping her paperback to the floor and tugging his book from his hands to put on the side table under the squat low-lit lamp. She lifted her skirts so fast he glimpsed white panties before she sat astride him and fanned out the material. Then she leaned forward and cupped his cheeks. Her kiss was so soft Nate wrapped his arms around her under her jumper. He needed to feel her skin.

"We're going to make a deal right here, right now. You listening?" she asked.

Nate nodded, tears welling at her determined, angry stare. He knew she wasn't angry at him, just at the feelings he'd voiced.

"I'm listening," he replied.

There wasn't a sound in the library aside from the grandfather clock ticking at a steady pace.

"There is no such thing as divorce between us. We're not going to talk about it. We argue we figure it out, but we're in this for life. I chose you because you settled me. You settle me so much I didn't know I was lost."

Tears dripped down her face, but she didn't appear to be crying. It was emotion leaking out. Nate leaned up and kissed her cheek and then her lips.

"I didn't realise how lonely I felt until I met you. I didn't realise how much I wanted to protect someone, hold them in my arms until you needed me," he said.

"I'm going to need you for the rest of my life. Our children will need both of us until they turn fifteen, and then we'll have ten years where they won't, but we'll secretly support them, anyway."

Daisy grinned at him with watery happy eyes.

"I love you, Daisy Hill," Nate said.

He flicked the clasp on her bra, then moved his hands to cup her naked breasts.

"And I love..."

Nate kissed her before she could moan too loudly as he pinched her nipples. She broke away, dropped her hands under her skirts, unbuckled his belt, and popped the button on his jeans.

He looked over his shoulder at the tall, ornately carved library door.

"Two can play your game," she whispered as she kissed him. "The door is locked, and I slid the bolt across. Even if someone comes with a key, they aren't getting in."

Nate lifted his hips so she could pull his jeans down, and then she pushed her panties to the side. In moments he was sheathed inside her.

His favourite place in the world. And she'd just said she wanted kids.

30

Imelda

Late February brought warmer days, but still, the nights were chilly. It had been three months since she'd dumped the boxes for her children to sort through and begin preparations for running Copper Island. Christmas and New Year had been about celebrations. Isobel's first Christmas, and as a family, they were all together for the first time in nearly thirty years.

Imelda had cried so hard on Christmas night. Grateful she'd found the courage to come back. Everyone had squashed into her parents' house on Boxing Day to eat leftover turkey and gorge on sweets. It was handy her father was a butcher.

Luke was getting frustrated that he couldn't marry Freya immediately and threw glances at Daisy and Nate across the table at family dinner time. Daisy was pregnant, and so was Erica. Heidi was far along and showing proudly, which added to his exasperation of being last to marry and father a child.

Imelda found great joy living in the fifth cottage beside her children. They were raising families, and she would be a part of that.

She was wrapped up warm under a fleecy blanket, reading a book mid-afternoon, when an alarm sounded on her phone. It was their version of a bat signal.

Imelda sighed heavily, closed the paperback she was reading and tossed it onto the glass-topped coffee table. She swung her legs from the sofa cushions and placed them carefully and slowly on the floor. It was her way of buying time to settle the anger brewing.

The alarm was Bailey's notification that Cynthia was on her way.

Clutching the edge of the cushions, she bowed her head, closing her eyes. Then she swung her head to look across the lawns. Striding across was a spritely Cynthia. Even at eighty-one, she showed no signs of fatigue.

When Cynthia was near enough that it was no coincidence where she was heading, Imelda stood up and shed the fleece blanket and draped it over the back of the outdoor sofa. The winter sun had some heat, but it didn't stop the shiver when Imelda focused on Freddie's sister.

Imelda didn't consider herself violent, but she could cheerfully throttle the woman. Cynthia's pinched face came nearer. Shrewd eyes narrowed in on her, but Imelda resisted the urge to flee.

Her children would protect her, and God love them. All eight of them were striding out onto the lawn behind Cynthia to play an impromptu game of frisbee.

"Cynthia," Imelda said, frostier than she intended.

"Imelda. You're back."

"We both know you knew the moment I stepped foot on Copper Island months ago," Imelda replied, coming to the opening of her patio and stepping onto the path.

She didn't want Cynthia in her home.

A tabby kitten pushed between Imelda's ankles, looked up at Cynthia and hissed. Imelda suppressed the urge to laugh. The kitten was Daisy and Nate's new pet, but the cat seemed to prefer Imelda's home.

Cynthia glared at the creature and then looked back at Imelda's face.

"I was a little shocked that they did not invite me to Daisy's wedding," Cynthia replied, then cleared her throat.

Imelda laughed humourlessly, which drew the attention of her children. When she stopped, they kept throwing the frisbee around. Most times, it landed on the floor as they were busy looking her way.

"You're shocked? Shocked? You're shocked that she doesn't want you at her wedding after being locked in a room with no food for two days? Christ, you are a piece of work."

"Well, at least I wasn't the only one not invited. The child didn't invite her brothers."

"And that was your fault, too," Imelda yelled. "All the heartache this family has suffered is from your actions. Even your own misery was because you were a scared bully."

"I'll remind you that you are on Turner land," Cynthia haughtily cautioned.

"And I'm a fucking Turner. Right to the end. You cannot take that away from me. I married a Turner, and I bore the children that will take over this island and do a better job of making it prosper than you ever did."

"I did the best I could. Father never left me any instructions after Freddie died."

"Karma is for the next life, but it looks like it made an exception for you. You should've been a nicer person, then perhaps you would have had a nicer life. How is vegetarian life going for you?"

Cynthia blanched at the comment.

"That's right. You're not the only one who has spies. I would never lower myself to your level and poison another living creature. What do you think you were going to gain by killing me?"

Without her clocking it, the frisbee game had inched nearer the rear of her cottage, and Teddy was the only one tossing the piece of plastic around. Erica held Isobel in her arms, swaying and distracting her from the tense vibe no doubt wafting out from their conversation.

"I wasn't trying to kill you," she whispered, twisting her sapphire ring.

"What did you think would happen when I got so ill? What do you feel when you know I missed out on my children's lives because you had this drive to be an heir? Now that you have the island, was it worth it?"

Imelda flung her arms out to the side in exasperation. She could feel her voice lifting as she spoke. Any answers she was given would be meaningless because Freddie would still be dead, and she still would have lost out on decades with her children.

Cynthia remained quiet, looking up to the eaves of the cottage and then back to Imelda. It struck her that Cynthia was a different woman from the one who had walked across the grass to see her.

"What do you want? Why are you here?" Imelda demanded.

Silence came again. Cynthia's lips folded in like she was bracing herself. Then it dawned on Imelda what Cynthia wanted.

Needed.

"You want me to forgive you," she said.

Cynthia's eyes snapped up to Imelda's face. There was barely a nod, but she saw it.

"I forgive you," Imelda said boldly.

A collective gasp went up from the peanut gallery. Imelda swiped her eyes along the row of her children and their loved ones and nodded to them. Like a formation of soldiers, they all turned and marched off in a line. Daisy looked back as Nate grabbed her hand, and Imelda smiled at her daughter. She nodded and then turned her gaze back to Cynthia Turner, who seemed to shrink before her eyes.

"You will give me and my children the freedom to roam this estate. You'll hand over the reins of Copper Island within the next twelve months. You will do this openly and willingly and won't interfere with how Archer wants to set up the future of this island," Imelda said.

Cynthia opened her mouth to speak, but Imelda held up her hand.

"I know what is most precious to you, and that is the Turner name. If you don't do as I ask, I will take them away from Copper Island, and we'll set up a home elsewhere. You have proven through your actions that my four children are resourceful and can earn a living without the Turner name."

Imelda knew Freya wouldn't leave her family, and if Freya stayed, then Luke was staying. If Luke was staying, they were all staying. The same went for Heidi, but Cynthia didn't know that.

"We got a deal?" Imelda pushed.

There was a wave of relief in Cynthia's eyes when she nodded fully.

"I'll hand it over. Whenever Archer wants to meet with the lawyers, let Bailey know, and he'll arrange everything."

"That's settled. If you behave yourself, I'll see you have an invitation to Luke and Freya's wedding."

Cynthia's eyes widened.

"Thank you."

"It's more than you deserve. But I will not spend another moment of my life with resentment in my heart. You did what you did, and we can't reverse that. We can only make it better. Watching my children tiptoe around this place is heartbreaking. This is their legacy. It's about time they enjoyed it while they are young. I want their children to run around this place with no fear in their minds. It's the very least I can do for them."

"Understood," Cynthia said with conviction.

Imelda went to turn away and then turned back. "And another thing?"

"Yes?" Cynthia said a little too brightly.

"Put their names on the damn gravestones. We all know who is buried there."

Cynthia's head dropped, her chin touching her chest. Imelda heard the quiet sob before the woman turned and walked away. When she was halfway across the lawn, Imelda was swarmed with bodies around her that had walked out from her kitchen door. Daisy hugged her from behind, and Archer slung an arm around her shoulders. They must have gone through Daisy's home and let themselves in through her front door.

"You kicked ass, Mum," Luke said.

His arms were folded like Jason's stance as they watched

the elderly woman keep a swift pace as she walked back to Turner Hall.

"I think we're all free. I hope you're ready to take over Turner Hall. At least there are eight of you to take the burden. It was too much for Freddie," Imelda said.

She burst into tears, her legs buckling, but Archer caught her and gently put her on the sofa. Erica bundled Isobel onto her lap, and the gurgling baby chuckled and patted her grandmother's cheek.

"I am so excited to see my grandchildren grow up," Imelda said, looking at them all one by one. "It's going to be bedlam, but I'm going to love every moment."

"Can I please get married next week?" Luke said.

"No," came the chorus of replies.

His pout started a ripple of laughter.

"I'll get the kettle on," Freya said and headed back inside.

Heidi followed, as did everyone else apart from Archer.

He sat down next to his mum and tickled his daughter.

"Are you okay, Mum?"

"Yeah," she said, sniffing back tears. "You all call me Mum, and that's enough for me."

Archer wrapped his arm around her shoulders and brought her in for a hug.

"And Granny," he said.

o

Thank you for reading Electric Kiss, the fourth and final book in *The Turners of Copper Island* series. I can't tell you how happy it makes me you spent the time reading it.

Cynthia's story is available if you want to read the villain's story. It starts decades ago when she's set to marry

Jonathan Cranford, but her father has other plans. And it ends right up to Archer coming back to the Island in Reckless Kiss.

If you want to keep up to date with my future releases, sales, and giveaways, click HERE for my newsletter.

READER MESSAGE

Daisy and Nate's story in Electric Kiss was so heartwarming to write. I fell in love with these two as I do with all my characters. They were so lonely for different reasons but being together was all they needed. And a good book.

If you like stand alone novels where the main character has to navigate difficult family members while they find their happy ever after, then check out THE STRANGER'S VOICE. I've put a snipper on the following page.

If you get time, a rating or review would be amazing.

Want to keep up to date with my news? Then click HERE to subscribe to my newsletters. All news goes to email subscribers first.

Take care

Grace

You can find me online, search for GraceHarperBooks

FOREWORD

Sensorineural hearing loss not only changes our ability to hear quiet sounds, but it also reduces the quality of the sound that is heard, meaning that individuals with this type of hearing loss will often struggle to understand speech. Once the cochlea hair cells become damaged, they will remain damaged for the rest of a person's life. Therefore sensorineural hearing loss is irreversible and cannot be cured – at least at the present time.

Each person's experience of losing their hearing at an early age is different. My hearing loss has been a long journey of acceptance.

I wanted to write a love story where two people find each other and don't care about each other's hidden imperfections. This is a work of fiction, of a girl meeting a boy. She falls in love, terrified that he won't accept her hidden imperfection. He falls in love with her with the same fear.

I hope you enjoy Adaline and Callum's story.

Grace

31

ADALINE

The problem with squeezing one more internet search before I left the flat meant I ran late for appointments. I liked to maximise every waking hour with the aid of caffeine. It would be no surprise to Steph, but today I was super late. The chain on my bike clanged as I peddled up the hill to the train station. I could have cycled down the hill and across to Brighton Pier, but I was a sucker for the shortcut. In my haste to get to Steph, I'd caught the hem of my summer dress in the chain. Steph Parkins, my best friend oozed style and sophistication. Making an effort for Steph meant that I wore a dress when I met up with her. The blame from my chewed-up dress was all Steph's, she would disagree but it wouldn't stop me from telling her. I yanked out the pale-yellow material, instead of back peddling for my dress to come free of my bike. A sample of the material intertwined through the groove of the links. The bike didn't sound right, but I couldn't hang around to fix the chain, it would be the fastest way to get to Steph. There wasn't enough time to go home, change, and then get a bus. Hitching the skirt of the dress into the elastic of my knickers, I peddled faster down the main street from Brighton train station to the seafront. Heading to the new tourist viewing platform, I avoided the tourists who didn't know they didn't walk in the cycle lane. I refused to attach a bell on the handlebars, I wasn't six years old. I much preferred to yell at them to get out of the way.

Runaway children and footballs hampered my path. Cursing three times under my breath and out loud a few times I made it to the cafe half an hour late. Two men were unchaining their bikes, giving me a spot on the bike rack outside the cafe. I waved over at Steph who wore an enormous white floppy hat and large sunglasses. She was sitting under an umbrella looking fantastic in her chic French attire. Her sense of style astounded me, she wore wide-legged white trousers and a loose fitting white blouse. I had an old dress with grease stains thanks to my bike, with a rip. I felt inferior being within twenty feet of her. It was a good job I adored her or I'd turn around and run away until I learned fashion sense.

Locking up my bike, I took off my helmet and pushed the stray hairs back into my bun. I greeted Steph with a cuddle, grabbing harder when she tried to pull away.

"You look like a movie star sitting here," I told her and fell into the seat next to her.

"For a film star, I was on time," her playful retort came with a wink and a nudge. I could see she'd finished the green tea in front of her. The pages of the open paperback fluttered in the breeze coming in from the sea.

"I'm sorry, this week has been an epic fuck up, does this place sell wine?" I said. Pulling the menu that stood upright between the salt and pepper to glance at what they served. Putting my helmet on the floor and my bag on the table. Searching for my purse, I tried to catch the eye of the waitress at the same time. Succeeding in neither, I gave up and told Steph about my hateful ex-tenant.

"I located my big girl knickers and go into the flat. It's a state. Everything he left, he had smashed to pieces. So, Jeff fucking Brightey not only hasn't paid three months rent, I now have to find someone to repair the damage he's caused. Plus, I have to find a new tenant." By the end of my mini-rant, the waitress had taken my order. Steph had rammed her fist against her mouth to stop her smirk from morphing into a full-on belly laugh. She wasn't mean, she thought my rants were so funny, and never took my grumblings to heart. Steph never swore, but lately, I couldn't go four sentences without using the words *fuck* or *shit*. Ignoring the mirth that danced in her eyes, I soldiered on with my story.

"I dragged the few personal items Jeff had left behind in a box and put it out the back next to the skip."

"Whose skip?" she asked. Her words slow and deliberate, questioning if I had dumped a whole load of rubbish in someone else's skip.

Now I had her attention, she took a sip of my latte and gestured for me to carry on with what I was saying.

"I can order you a coffee, it's no hardship, we don't have to share."

My sarcasm laced my words, but I ended up laughing. Steph had given up caffeine after an article she'd read in a magazine. This was week two and Elliott, her husband had already switched the decaf coffee in the house to full strength. He loved her, but she was a little testy without her caffeine. He preferred his balls where they were.

"I ordered a skip," I said and pulled the latte away from her reach. "It arrived this morning. I can throw Jeff's stuff over the balcony and into the skip, it will save time trooping up and down the stairs all day. It helps with the rage I feel for my ex-tenant, to fling the broken pieces of furniture over the wall and hear it crash into the skip. I imagine I am throwing his body off a cliff into the ocean. The tide would be out, and there are sharp, spiky rocks to soften his fall."

Steph let out a chuckle that ended up as a snort. To cover her embarrassment, she closed her novel.

"You've thought about it, I see. When was the last time you saw Jeff?"

"About a month ago," I said. I couldn't pin down the last time I had seen him. I'd heard him plenty of times banging about the flat. He had a heavy footfall, thundering down the back stairs and then the inevitable slam of the front door. I didn't let him come through the shop to get out. As far as he knew there wasn't any access to the shop. Every day I made sure that the door to the interior stairs had the bolt in place from the other side. I came into the shop to work to avoid him. The only way in while he was renting was through the front door of the shop. Jeff had keys to the door on the side street, next to the backyard door. He wasn't allowed in there either. It took five days after he moved in for me to distrust him. I was too chicken to kick him out.

"Do you know any carpenters?" I asked to change the subject. I needed to get the flat back into a habitable state to rent out again. Every week it was vacant was a week I had to find the money to pay the bills.

"I'll ask Elliott if he knows anyone," she said and tried to hide her smirk again.

"Thanks," I said.

I didn't want to know the reason behind her smile, but it always meant she was up to mischief.

"I've changed the locks to the back entrance and his flat. If he turns up, then he's not getting into the flat." I took a sip of latte after my rant.

"You're well rid of him. Let's hope he's gone for good and didn't want the stuff he left behind in the flat."

"Most of his personal stuff was his record collection. They are all in a metal box with enough clasps to keep out a pirate, marauding on the high seas. I tried to break it open, but just snapped a nail for my efforts."

"Sod him. Does this mean you haven't found a tenant? Steph asked me, she concentrated on my reactions. I made a fish impression, trying to break her scrutiny, she only lasted thirty seconds before breaking into fits of giggles. I raised my eyebrows still making the fish impression with my lips. My cheeks hollowed out, and I increased the tempo of my lips moving up and down. Steph threw her cloth napkin at me, and I grinned.

"Why do you want to know?"

Leaning forward, I widened my eyes wide to raise my eyebrows towards my hairline. Steph had a plan of action, her sheepish looking face said it all. She had never cared to help me in the past to get a tenant. I put an advert in the local paper, spend an entire day in a pub interviewing the prospective tenants, while getting drunk.

I threw her napkin back at her, folded my arms under my breasts and waited for her to answer.

Steph straightened up and took a deep breath. "Elliott's best friend has just come home from overseas. He's staying with us, but after a day, he feels uncomfortable imposing on us. We'd have him there forever, but he feels as we've been married less than a year, we should have the freedom to have sex wherever and whenever we feel like it. He thinks him being around will dampen our sex life.

"That's considerate. Is he good looking?" I asked. A hot guy moving into the flat opposite mine would be disastrous. I'd never met a handsome man who wasn't an arsehole.

"No, I don't think so," she frowned and looked up to the sky for divine help. "No, definitely not handsome."

"You're a shit liar. Is he rich?" I thought rich, handsome men were the worst kind. I should know, my university was full of them. Steph had fixed me up on a few dates with her friends when I came home for the holidays. All of them stunning in the looks department and had a decent bank balance. All of them rude, arrogant, and self-centred. I had no interest in those kinds of men. Give me a poor, plain man, any day of the week. So long as he had rugby player thighs.

"Um," she pondered this question, looking left and right. Who, she thought would help her with the question I did not know, unless she hoped the seagulls sauntering around our table knew the answer.

"Let me make this easier. Is he richer than the Beckhams?"

"Um," she paused again.

"Fuck off, Steph, you had to think about that? Why the hell would you try to get him to rent the flat if he's minted?" Irritated for a moment, I took a swig of my latte, only to find it freezing cold. Politeness dictated that I swallow the liquid.

"He's down to earth, normal like you, Elliott, and me. You won't regret letting him move in, I promise. You'd never know he is wealthy, he's not flash. He drives an old beat-up van and has no home to call his own."

Steph fluttered her eyelashes, blowing me smooch kisses and clasping her hands in a begging motion.

"I want to interview him first, if he passes my strict questions, then he can move into Jeff's flat. But, the flat is a state. Jeff left it in a real mess, the doors are hanging off the hinges in the kitchen, the carpet needs replacing. None of which I can afford. The shop is a money pit too. I need to sell a decent comic to finish the renovations."

"Did I mention, he's a carpenter?"

"Shut up," I said a little too loud for the ladies on the adjacent table.

Steph nodded, happy that she'd at last found his unique selling point. That simple fact might go in his favour. I hope he isn't a carpenter with his arse hanging out of his trousers when he bends down to work. Unless he looks like a rugby player, then I'd just stare at him all day.

"Give him my address and tell to come and see me the day after tomorrow at 10am. Tell him, if he's late, he's lost his chance."

Steph jumped up and hugged me, planting a big wet kiss on my cheek. She glanced at me, gauging my mood, seeing I wasn't glaring, she sat back down on her chair. Raising her eyebrows and straightening the sugar bowl to align with the salt and pepper pots she spoke again.

"I need a favour Adaline, please don't say no."

Her earnest plea had me silenced, she never asked me a favour. I would do anything for her.

"The organiser for the Charity Gala Ball has walked away, something to do with the chairwoman of the charity being too demanding. You have the organisational skills I would die to have. Please, will you step in and help?"

Steph was a part-time bookkeeper. She did the accounts for a charity that Elliott's company supported. The widow of the man who started the electronics firm that Elliott ran started the charity after he died. She'd gone to Nairobi on holiday and came back with plans to build a school. I'd never met her or her husband when he was alive. Steph knew she was asking a lot of me with this request. The organising part would be a breeze. Listening was not my forte, listening to people in person or on the phone was a problem. Unless I could organise the whole thing by email. If I had my way, the only people who I would talk to would be Steph and Elliott.

"Why don't you hire someone else? I'm not the best person for the job."

"I can't find anyone local that will take it up with such short notice. Event organisers cost a small fortune, and I know you'd do it for nothing."

"When is the Gala Ball?"

"Two weeks, tomorrow," Steph had the good grace to grimace after she uttered the words.

"Fuck off, no way can I organise a charity ball in two weeks, I would need at least three months. How much progress is there?"

"Three months? You could do it in three months? Well, I may have got the dates wrong, it's a Winter ball, late November."

"You," I didn't know what to call her as I waggled my finger at her. My screwed-up eyes scrutinised her angelic face feigning innocence, but no horrible words came to mind. Steph and Elliott saved me from the horror of my parents when they kicked me out of my home. "Ok, I'll do it. Three months is plenty of time."

"The organiser has disappeared. She's not answering our calls, so we have to start again. We have high-profile people coming, potential large donations. Elliott's mate is running in the Brighton Triathlon and already had five grand in sponsorship. One or two celebrities and a bunch of business men and women will donate. I wouldn't beg, but organising is your super power."

I didn't want to do it. Steph did not understand what it

would take out of me to arrange everything, but our friendship meant everything.

"The ugly rich potential flatmate runs marathons for fun?"

"Is that the only thing you're focussing on Adaline?"

"No," I said. I was hoping he had rugby player thighs. "Fine, tell me more about this demanding chairwoman?"

"She's always been gracious and kind, so not sure why our organiser quit. Maybe they clashed, a personality thing. I know no one else that could pull this off with success. You organised so many of these things at Uni."

She fell silent, letting me contemplate what she was asking. Steph knew I would say yes, but still gave me the time to say no. She had already saved my ass with a prospective new tenant, which allowed me to pay the bills, the least I could do was repay the favour.

"Ok, I'll do it, where is it being held?"

"At the Empire Hotel," she said and pointed over my shoulder at the grand red brick hotel overlooking the seafront. "I can give you the details for the event manager. I'll give you the password to the charity email account that deals with this event. You can find all the emails from the suppliers in there. I'm so grateful Adaline, you are saving the charity's event."

"I have a condition," I said, resolute in my ultimatum.

"Name it," she grinned, leaning forward to take in my condition.

"I'm not attending, I'll organise it, stay until the first guests arrive, and then I'll hand over to one of the charity trustees on the night."

"That's a shame," she said and pouted. "I understand, maybe you'll change your mind once you get to grips with the event. Maybe there will be a man in your life, and you'll want to bring him as a date." Steph said with a certainty that scared me.

I wouldn't change my mind, the last thing I wanted was to attend a gala ball with a room full of people I didn't know. At least with the email account, I could correspond with the attendees and charity members without having to speak with them.

"It's too stressful to go, too many opportunities to misread people and to look like a complete fucking fool. I'll be wishing I could run away the whole time."

"I get it, I can't imagine what it's like to lose your hearing. You're superwoman to know how to lip read the way you can."

She was genuine with her concern, not in the least bit patronising. I'd shared with Steph and Elliott my inability to hear most people's words. I couldn't hear female voices and the majority of men's voices. It was like I had sunk to the bottom of the swimming pool, I could hear muffled sounds but not the words. It was something about the pitch. When the doctor explained it, I wasn't listening, on purpose. There were few people I could hear. Brian Blessed was one person I could hear. I had hidden myself away in a bar not far from the shop, searching the internet for my latest customer. Some time after my second pint, a booming voice, clear as day drifted over from the other side of the pub. No one else had that ability since that day.

I'd rather suffer in silence and use text messages over talking. Steph and Elliott made sure they were facing me when they spoke so I could understand them. School and University didn't affect me. Teachers and Professors talked at me from the front of the class. Learning to lip read at a kid was hard work but the determination to hide my problem from the world and my parents spurred me to learn every technique I could. I saw a doctor while at University in America. The hearing aids he gave me still sat in the red velvet-lined box in the bottom drawer of my wardrobe. I was sure they wouldn't work, and I knew for sure my hearing had worsened since his appointment.

Steph clasped my hand that rested around my mug and squeezed my fingers.

"Thank you for understanding, I better get going. Say hello to Elliott for me." I said and got up from my seat, Steph stood too and hugged me hard. She waited until I broke the embrace and faced her.

"Please come for dinner during the week, Elliott misses you."

I hugged her again, leaving her at the table, she resumed her seat and watched me battle with the long thick chain for my bike. The lock was the most expensive thing I owned apart from the shop, more expensive than the bike itself. At seventy-four years old, my neighbour declared that the streets of Brighton were too dangerous for her to cycle. She said the double-decker buses were making it their mission to run her over. One Sunday morning, she knocked on my door and presented me with her bike.

The bus drivers could get impatient as they have a timetable to stick to. They could get a little close to my back tyre. I understood why she worried about her reaction time. The bike was the perfect mode of transport, I go everywhere on it. My car is an old classic that sits in my garage because I can't afford to run it. The bike saves me a fortune in bus and train fares.

Once the coiled lock was in the saddle bag, I gave Steph one last wave and headed along the seafront, back to my shop.

ABOUT THE AUTHOR

I was born and raised in Wales, in a sleepy town just outside Cardiff. Developing a love of stationery at a very early age, I still can't pass a pen shop without nipping in for a quick look around.

Writing and publishing since 2012, I have many books in my back catalogue, all in the Romance genre. They range from Rock Star Romance to Small Town Romance to Family Sagas. Be warned, the stories have a steamy heat level!

In a nutshell?
21st Century Romance—Writing about understated powerful women. Understated love stories with a powerful message, each and every time.

ALSO BY GRACE HARPER
THE TURNERS OF COPPER ISLAND SERIES

The Turners are coming home and they're looking for love.

Reckless Kiss ~ Stolen Kiss ~ Lipstick Kiss ~ Electric Kiss ~ The Turners of Copper Island – Cynthia's Story

THE DEVOTED MEN SERIES

Three men, two brothers and their best friend find love in the most unexpected places. They are only looking to marry once and forever.
Charming Olivia ~ Loving Lilly ~ Tempting Angie

THE THIS LOVE SERIES

A rockstar romance spanning the years. A woman coming to terms with survivor's guilt and a man who will never give up on her.
THIS LOVE ~ THIS LOVE ALWAYS ~ THIS LOVE FOREVER ~ FIVE CHANCES

THE RED & BLACK SERIES

A record label series. Each of the record label owners and senior staff have their story told. Intrigue, revenge, rival record labels, and a whole lotta heat.
Charcoal Notes ~ Crimson Melodies ~ raven acoustics ~ cardinal lyrics ~ Onyx Keys ~ Vermillion Chords ~ Inky Rhapsodies ~ Magenta Symphonies ~ White Wedding

THE TALBOT GIRLS NOVELLAS
FESTIVE, SMALL-TOWN NOVELLAS TO WARM YOUR HEART.

Stranded at New Year ~ His Christmas Surprise ~ Under the Mistletoe ~ Snowflakes at Dawn ~ A Holiday Wish

STANDALONE NOVELS

THE STRANGER'S VOICE ~ HOLLYWOOD SPOTLIGHT ~ THE GIRL UPSTAIRS ~ FASHION ~ SERENADE

Sign up to my email list HERE

ACKNOWLEDGMENTS

My husband of over two decades is my ever love. Each story I write has a little bit of him in the hero.

Many people have supported me over the years with my novel writing. They should all be mentioned in every book as they shaped the writer I am today. I am thankful that I have a team behind me who keep me straight and make me laugh.

Not everyone helps on every book, but there are still there, cheerleading from the sidelines.

No one will love my characters as much as I do, but when I see a review that accurately says what I feel when I write about them, it is the most satisfying feeling in the world.

I am grateful to my readers. May you keep enjoying my books.

I also want the thank the makers of *Maltesers*. Without them, these books would not be published.

Printed in Great Britain
by Amazon